"What am I going to do about you, Kara?"

His tone was subdued and so sincere that his question caught her by surprise. "What do you mean?"

"I can't stay away from you."

"You seem to be doing a fine job of it," she said quietly, but without malice.

"I know it seems that way, but you don't know how hard it's been."

She was skeptical. "We just danced together, but after tonight, how will it be between us? Will you still ignore me in the halls? Will you duck into the nearest open door whenever you see me coming?"

He turned his head, and she saw his jaw clench. She thought he might walk away, but instead he asked, "What's between you and Vince?"

Other Bantam books you will enjoy:

I'LL BE SEEING YOU, by Lurlene McDaniel

MOURNING SONG, a One Last Wish novel
by Lurlene McDaniel

WHEN HAPPILY EVER AFTER ENDS
by Lurlene McDaniel

DON'T DIE, MY LOVE by Lurlene McDaniel

ALL THE DAYS OF HER LIFE
by Lurlene McDaniel

BORROWED CHILDREN by George Ella Lyon

THE YEAR WITHOUT MICHAEL
by Susan Beth Pfeffer

WORDS BY HEART by Ouida Sebestyen

ONE LAST WISH

Lurlene McDaniel

A Time to Die

BANTAM BOOKS
NEW YORK • TORONTO • LONDON • SYDNEY • AUCKLAND

RL 5, age 10 and up

A TIME TO DIE
A Bantam Book / May 1992

The Starfire logo is a registered trademark of Bantam Books, a division of Bantam Doubleday Dell Publishing Group, Inc. Registered in U.S. Patent and Trademark Office and elsewhere.

ISBN 0-553-29809-7

Published simultaneously in the United States and Canada

Bantam Books are published by Bantam Books, a division of Bantam Doubleday Dell Publishing Group, Inc. Its trademark, consisting of the words "Bantam Books" and the portrayal of a rooster, is Registered in U.S. Patent and Trademark Office and in other countries. Marca Registrada. Bantam Books, 1540 Broadway, New York, New York 10036.

PRINTED IN THE UNITED STATES OF AMERICA

OPM 0 9 8

This book is dedicated
to the memory of
Karen Leigh Fleming,
October 6, 1967–February 20, 1991,
a victim of cystic fibrosis.

One

"Come on, Kara. Stop fidgeting. I'm almost through with your treatments," Christy Lawrence said as she thumped on Kara Fischer's back.

Kara stopped squirming. She knew that Christy, her respiratory therapist, was doing her job as quickly as possible, but it didn't make Kara any happier about the procedure. "Sorry," Kara apologized. "I'm just anxious to get out of here. I wish I was home already."

Christy's cupped hands beat in a constant rhythm against Kara's back for two minutes, then moved to press against her chest. "Just another ten minutes and you can start packing."

Kara grimaced and coughed, clearing from her chest the thick phlegm that the therapeutic pounding had dislodged. "You know how I hate being in the hospital," Kara said. "It's a good thing Dr. McGee said I was well enough to go home today, or I might just have checked out without his approval. School starts next week."

"I know you're longing for school to start. I was like that when I was your age," Christy said. "Most sixteen-year-olds have to be dragged back to the classroom. That's why we need to finish up your treatments—so that you'll be in good shape for the first day. Okay—upsy-daisy."

Christy paused while Kara coughed. Then Kara bent over a mound of pillows on the floor of her hospital room. She felt the rush of blood to her head. Kara especially hated the treatments that had to be administered while she was upside down. She told herself that she should be used to it by now. She'd been receiving postural drainage therapy—"thumps," kids like her called them—two to three times a day for her cystic fibrosis since she was three years old. The vibrations from the therapeutic pounding helped to dislodge the thick mucus that clogged her lungs.

"I'm not giving you a hard time," Kara insisted. "You know I love you. It's CF I hate."

"I'd say you got over this lung infection pretty quickly. Only two weeks in the hospital this time. That's good."

"Even two hours is too much," Kara grumbled after inhaling a dose of aerosol antibiotic mist from the mask Christy handed her. "And I lost all the weight I worked so hard to gain this summer, too."

Christy helped Kara sit upright. "You're still adorable. Listen, have a milk shake on your way home. My treat!"

The mere mention of food turned Kara's stomach. If only she had an appetite. Eating was no fun these days—it seemed like a chore. She coughed hard and spit into a small basin. *Gross.* CF was so gross. Over the years, Kara had devised techniques for controlling her coughing and perpetual throat clearing when around other people, but during her thumps, she tried her best to clear her bronchial passages of the thick, choking mucus that was the curse of CF. "Are we through?" she asked, wiping perspiration from her forehead.

"I just want to put you on the dilator to measure your lung elasticity. While we're doing this test, I've got a favor to ask."

"A favor from me? Just name it." Kara sat in a nearby chair while Christy set the dials of the portable machine and placed the end of the tubing in Kara's mouth.

"Now that I've got you where you can't say no," Christy teased, "I want to tell you about my brother, Eric. Have I mentioned him to you?"

Kara knew a lot about Christy because throughout the two years Christy had been her therapist, they had become close friends. She knew that her twenty-four-year-old friend, with the soft brown hair and green eyes, had grown up in Texas, had moved to Nashville and received her training there, and now lived alone in an apartment not too far from Kara's neighborhood.

Whenever Christy couldn't afford to go home for the holidays, Kara's parents invited her over. They had all grown dependent on one another, not just because of Kara's CF, but because they genuinely liked each other. In some ways, Christy had become the sister Kara always wished she'd had.

Kara also knew that Christy longed to be a doctor, but though they never discussed it, Kara suspected that money was a big problem. Christy was smart and talented enough to get into the medical school at Vanderbilt, but becoming a doctor was a long and expensive endeavor. Secretly, Kara was relieved. If Christy ever went back to school, Kara would lose her as a therapist.

Christy adjusted the dial as Kara puffed deeply into the flexible tube. "Actually, I'm coming to the aid of my parents. Eric's your age. He plans to come live with me this school year and will be going to Central High, same as you. I need you to keep an eye out for him."

Christy removed the tube from between Kara's lips and jotted notes on a medical chart. "Forty-five percent," she said with a frown. "I'm afraid this last infection's taken its toll."

Kara hardly heard the comments about her medical condition. "Why's he living with you?" She was brimming with questions about Christy's brother.

"Let's just say he needed a change from Houston." Christy answered while she busied herself with the equipment.

"Does he have two heads or something?"

Christy smiled. "No . . . Eric's had some clashes with Mom and Dad. We decided everybody could use a little vacation from each other, so he'll move in with me for the school year. Can you introduce him around so that he won't feel like a stranger? He's really a pretty great guy, when he wants to be."

Kara was surprised by Christy's evasive tone. "How will I recognize him? Do you have a picture of him?"

Christy dug in her pocket and pulled out a school-size photo. Kara saw the family resemblance instantly. Eric was smiling. He had gorgeous blue eyes and shaggy brown hair that fell across his forehead, and he was *definitely* good-looking. "I'll be able to pick him out in a crowd," she said as nonchalantly as possible. "But he shouldn't have any trouble fitting right in. He looks perfectly harmless."

"Anything you can do to make him feel less like a stranger would be a big help. Changing schools in his junior year could be a drag—even though I know he wants to come here." Christy glanced at her watch. "I'm running behind. Listen, tell your mother I can resume our regular schedule as soon as school starts, if that's okay. Now, don't forget that milk shake on your way home, and I'll see you soon."

Kara nodded. The regular schedule consisted of her parents' administering her postural drainage therapy first thing in the morning and last thing at night. Christy came to Kara's home for her treatments in the late afternoon. Kara hated the routine, but at least she had Christy. Besides, the clearer she kept her lungs, the better chance she had of avoiding infections and staying out of the hospital. "I'm going to pack up my stuff and be all ready when Mom gets here during her lunch hour."

Christy paused at the doorway. "Vince wants you to stop by to see him before you go home."

Kara smiled. "Don't worry. I wouldn't leave without saying good-bye to my buddy Vince."

Two

CHRISTY WAVED AS she dashed off, and Kara finished packing her small suitcase. She headed down the hall toward Vince's room. She paused in the doorway and peeked inside. Seventeen-year-old Vince Chapman lay on the bed, his eyes closed. An IV line was attached to the back of his hand, and a plastic oxygen mask stretched across his nose and mouth.

Kara tiptoed to his bedside. She watched his chest rise and fall, hearing the familiar rattle of congestion deep inside his lungs. Vince had CF also, and was a patient of Dr. McGee's. They had first met when she was twelve and he thirteen. The community of CF teenagers was small, even in a city the size of Nashville. Kara considered it fortunate that she and Vince should end up attending the same high school.

Kara had contracted her current lung infection in mid-August. One week later, Vince had been afflicted, too. The major difference was that Kara had responded well to the latest round of antibiotics and bronchodilators—Vince hadn't.

Kara studied Vince's face. He'd lost weight and looked gaunt and pale. Bright spots of color on his cheeks told her he was still fighting a fever. She'd almost decided to let him sleep and return to visit later when his eyelids opened. She smiled down at him and was rewarded by his smile in return. "Hi," she whispered. "How're you feeling?"

Vince lifted the mask off his face. "Better now that you're here." His voice sounded raspy.

"I'll bet you say that to all the girls."

"Sure. I mean there're so many in my life." Kara appreciated his sentiment. She, too, had no one special in her life. CF was a real turnoff in the dating scene. "Are you out of here?" Vince asked.

"Dr. McGee sprang me this morning. I just finished my treatment with Christy, and now I'm waiting for my mom to come and get me."

"I guess you'll be able to start school on time."

"Yes." She felt sorry for him, knowing he wouldn't. "You'll be back in no time yourself," she added.

His dark eyes looked defeated. "It's getting harder and harder to make a comeback."

Kara felt a flicker of fear, knowing he was talking about more than returning to school. "You'll do it. I'll save you a place in the cafeteria."

With effort, Vince made a face. "No need to threaten me."

She laughed and squeezed his hand. "I promised Dr. McGee I'd put on ten pounds by Christmas. It was my bargaining chip for blowing this joint. We can go out for hot fudge sundaes with Christy." Christy was Vince's therapist, too.

Vince's gaze traveled over her face tenderly. "I think you're beautiful, Kara."

"Nice try, Chapman, but I know the truth. I'm four foot ten and weigh eighty pounds. I'm skinny and ugly and"—she held out her hands—"and my fingers look funny." The clubbed appearance of her fingertips was typical of CF victims. She disliked her hands and tried not to draw attention to them.

Vince lifted his arm, pulling the IV line taut and touched the tip of his clubbed finger to hers. "ET phone home," he said.

"I'll phone you every day," she promised, knowing firsthand how long and lonely the days were in the hospital.

"Will you come visit me once school starts?"

"Of course. I'm supposed to get my driver's license *if* Mom and Dad don't chicken out. Honestly, my folks treat me like I'm still a kid." She made a face.

"When you get your license, take me for a ride, all right?"

"Anywhere special?"

"How about Hawaii?"

"Small problem. There's an ocean between us and Hawaii."

A smile flickered on his lips. "Look, if you're always going to make up an excuse . . ."

"Sorry. You're right. When we hit California, we'll sell the car and buy a boat."

"Let's take a ship. How about the *Love Boat*? We can stand by the rail and watch the moon on the water."

"Sounds like a dream."

"And when we get to the islands, we'll lie on the white sand and eat pineapple and poi and watch the sunset."

She smoothed a lock of his black hair, wishing such dreams could really come true for them. Maybe that's why she and Vince talked and joked about their getaway so much. They both knew it was impossible. Kara's parents would take her on a vacation anywhere, but she didn't want to go under the conditions her illness dictated. She wished she could see the world without the daily routine of CF. The threat of lung infections and the fear of being away from her medical support system were ever present. "It would be fun," she said. "Maybe someday, we'll get our wish."

"I wish I hadn't brought you down," Vince said, eyeing Kara's expression.

She brightened. "Wait a minute here . . . How many wishes are you making? Don't get greedy, you know."

Before he could answer, he was suddenly

racked by a coughing spasm. She grabbed a small basin from the bedside table and held it for him while he gagged. A trail of blood appeared in the bowl. "Should I ring for a nurse?"

He leaned back against the pillow, looking exhausted. "It's just a small bleed," he insisted. "The doc says it'll clear up."

Kara reached over and picked up Vince's oxygen mask and slipped it over his mouth. "You need to keep this on."

He took hold of her hand. "You *are* beautiful." His voice sounded muffled by the plastic shell of the mask.

Her heart went out to him. "Feel better, Vince. See you soon." Kara slipped from the room, suddenly eager to get outside into the fresh air and sunlight. She hated the hospital, the smells, the procedures, the confinement. She wanted to go home. She wanted to go back to school. She wished she could lead a normal life. "Being sick is the pits," she muttered under her breath. Being sick with cystic fibrosis was the worst.

"Kara: Earth to Kara. I don't think you've heard a word I've said about my class schedule." Elyse Shepherd sounded exasperated.

Kara was twisted in her chair, looking over the crowded cafeteria. Guiltily, she turned toward her friend. "Sorry. I'm on the lookout for Eric Lawrence, Christy's brother."

"That's all you've talked about for two days. You act as if it's some sort of sacred mission or something. Is he gorgeous or dog chow? You haven't said either way."

Kara nibbled at her sandwich without much appetite. "I told you—I'm just helping out like Christy asked me to."

"Maybe he'll need a girlfriend. I just happen to be available," Elyse said, flapping her eyelashes. "Or maybe you'll be his type—"

"'Fraid not. You know how much school I missed last year being sick. This year I aim to stay healthy and have a good time—you know, get to know more people, join some clubs."

"Kara, don't overdo it. Anyway, sometimes I think you try too hard to fit in around here."

"What's that supposed to mean?"

"I've watched you knock yourself out for people all the time, and they don't appreciate you. You should be more concerned about your health."

Kara knew that Elyse was trying to be helpful. After all, they'd been friends since junior high. But no matter how much Elyse tried, Kara realized, she could never truly understand Kara's illness. Not just the illness, but the feelings of helplessness and isolation that came along with it. "I'm going to *do* things this year," Kara insisted stubbornly.

"What about the spring dance committee last year? You worked and worked. I know you thought Kevin Wright would ask you to the dance, but he didn't, even though he flirted with you the whole time you were on the committee together," Elyse said.

Refusing to allow Elyse the satisfaction of knowing how much Kevin's rejection still meant, Kara retorted, "I worked on the dance because I wanted to. Kevin's at college now. It doesn't matter, anyhow." But deep down, it *did* matter. Kara remembered how Kevin had appeared so interested in her until he found out about her illness. He'd retreated so fast that there couldn't have been any other explanation.

"Kevin was a creep," Elyse muttered darkly.

With a swig of milk, Kara washed down the enzyme pills that she had to take before every meal to help her body digest food properly. "I made up my mind a long time ago not to let this illness get in my way. Only a few people know the secrets of my soul—"

"You mean Christy and Vince."

"Yes. And you understand plenty about me, too." She didn't add that because Elyse was healthy, she could *never* truly understand. "I want people to treat me as if I'm just a regular person." Kara leaned forward. "I think Eric just walked into the cafeteria. Look, over there by the side door."

Elyse followed Kara's gaze. "The guy does look lost. But then, on the first day, who doesn't?"

"I'll be back if he doesn't want to be bothered." Kara stood abruptly. She wove her way through the maze of tables and noisy groups of juniors who had the same lunch period. The closer she got, the more nervous she became and the more ridiculous she felt. Eric Lawrence was tall, probably over six feet. His hair was shaggier than in the photo she'd seen, but his eyes were the same startling bright blue.

He was standing, looking bored. "Are you Eric?" Kara asked.

He looked down at her and without smiling asked, "How'd you know my name?"

She tipped her head up toward him and, grinning, said, "I'm one of Central's 'it's-the-first-day-of-school-and-I-don't-know-a-living-soul-patrol.' I'm here to give you a friendly warning about the cafeteria food."

"You're too late," he said. "I've already had the food. Now how else can you be friendly? You aren't in any of my classes. I would have remembered. So back to question number one: How do you know my name?"

Kara glanced around. "We've got fifteen minutes before the end of lunch. Let's go outside, and we can talk."

Three

THE WARM SEPTEMBER sunshine felt good to Kara. She found an empty bench and plopped down. The air was fragrant with the scent of flowers, which she silently hoped wouldn't irritate her lungs and cause her to start coughing.

Eric sat beside her. "Is your mission really to ferret out loners and make them feel welcome?"

"I lied," she admitted, suddenly feeling nervous. "I know your sister, Christy."

"You're the one she told me about."

For a moment Kara's heart constricted. Had Christy mentioned that she had CF? Would it turn Eric off before she ever had a chance to get to know him? "Did she tell you that I'm really a princess under the spell of a wicked math teacher?"

He grinned at her. "She said she was paying you big bucks to be nice to me and check out what I'm up to. Believe me—" He fumbled for her name.

"Kara," she supplied. "Kara Fischer."

"Believe me, Kara, whatever she's paying isn't enough."

She laughed. Eric had appealed to her from the moment she'd seen his picture, and now, sitting next to him, she felt that her first instincts about him had been right. Eric was quick and fun and very good-looking. "Tell me, how does Nashville compare to Houston so far?"

"I've only been here four days. I haven't seen too much of the city. There are more hills than in Texas, and it's a lot greener, too." His gaze skimmed over her body. "Girls here are pretty, and so far, I like what I see."

She cleared her throat self-consciously. "And school?"

"School's school," he said with a shrug. "One's like any other to me."

"Was it hard to move right here in the middle of high school? Wasn't it hard to leave your friends?"

"Let's say I was highly motivated." He glanced away. "So, how do you know my sister?"

"I've had some health problems, and she's been my therapist." She hoped he wouldn't probe for details. She hoped he didn't *care* about her health problems.

"Is Christy any good?"

"The best. Your sister's totally terrific, but you must know that, or you wouldn't have moved in with her."

"Actually, Christy's a little too serious for me these days. We weren't all that close because of the eight years between us, but when she lived at home, we did have some good times together. I remember she used to take first aid courses, and she'd use me to practice on. She'd pretend I was an accident victim and bandage me from head to toe." He smiled as he remembered. "It was fun for a kid my age. She's really a frustrated doctor, you know. Too bad she could never go to medical school."

"You're staying then?" Kara asked.

"I plan to stick around and see how it goes between us." Eric eyed Kara and added, "If it gets too boring, you can help make my life more interesting."

His sexy gaze made Kara squirm self-consciously. "Central's one of the biggest schools in the city, so there's something for everyone. You'll like it here."

"Okay," he said with a shrug. "Because you said so, I'll give it a try." He plucked a flower from one of the planters. "How do you get home from school?"

"Usually, I take the bus."

"Why don't I give you a ride today?"

No boy had ever given her a ride home before. "You have a horse, or a car?" Kara kidded, because she didn't want him to guess she had so little experience with boys.

He laughed. "A fifty-seven Chevy. I drove it up from Houston, packed to the top with all my worldly goods."

She heard a sense of pride in his voice and determination, too. She felt a twinge of envy. She couldn't imagine having the freedom to climb into a car and drive alone through three states. She hated her CF and the prisoner it made of her. "I *would* like a ride home," she told him. "I could meet you here at three."

"Suits me." Eric stood just as the bell rang. "According to my class schedule, I have English last period."

"I have art," Kara said.

"Until three o'clock." He handed her the flower and walked away. Kara watched him, happier than she'd felt in weeks. Maybe it was going to be a good year after all. Maybe, for once, things might go her way—*if* she could stay healthy. She trotted off to retrieve her books and hurry to class.

Kara was about to go call her mother's office saying she'd missed her bus when Eric showed up, twenty minutes after three. He jogged up to her. "Sorry, but I had a slight mishap during English. I leaned too far back in my desk chair, and when I fell over, the teacher decided I'd done it on purpose. He gave me a detention."

Kara felt so relieved he hadn't stood her up that she barely heard his apology. "No problem." She felt a coughing fit coming on and discreetly turned her head and forced herself to take several deep breaths and swallow down the urge. She refused to give in to the building spasm, silently pleading, *Don't do this to me, lungs.* By the time they reached Eric's car, the sensation had passed.

"Here she is," Eric said as they came up beside a car that badly needed a paint job.

"It's—uh—a car, all right." Kara fumbled for a compliment for his vehicle. To her, it simply looked old.

"I know it needs some work." He held open the door, and she slid across a cream-color leather seat held together in places with tape. "One of my goals is to restore it to mint condition and sell it. Plenty of collectors will pay big bucks for this baby when she's all fixed up."

She directed him to her house and settled back, listening to the radio and watching the trees slip past. Even if the car was old and in need of work, she envied Eric. He was lucky to have such freedom. "There's my house," she told him, pointing to a sprawling ranch-style home, set far back on an expansive, rolling green lawn.

"Pretty nice," he said. "You always lived here?"

"All my life. My dad's an airline pilot, and my mom just started back to work full-time last year at an ad agency." Eric turned into the driveway, and Kara saw Christy's parked car. How could she have forgotten that she had a treatment that afternoon?

"Isn't that my sister's car?"

"Uh—yes. We've got a session," Kara explained hastily. "Nothing much. No big deal."

"Maybe I could hang around until you're finished."

"It'd be a drag. Besides, Christy doesn't like people around while she works. It's sort of distracting." *Disgusting, too,* Kara thought, crossing her fingers, hoping he'd accept her story without questions.

"You're probably right. Tell Christy I'll see her back at the apartment." He leaned across the seat and opened the door for her. His arm pressed against her felt muscular and warm. "If I can find my way home," he added with a laugh.

"Can you?" Kara was growing fidgety, fearful that Christy might step outside and invite her brother in.

"I'll manage," he assured her.

She stood beside his car. "Thanks for the ride."

"Sure."

Kara watched him back out of the driveway, holding her books and suppressing the urge to cough. The sunlight caught on the car's old chrome. Wistfully, she watched until he disappeared around a corner. With a sigh, Kara hoisted her books and started for the front door. Maybe she should have leveled about Christy's role in her life. But then again, if she had, Eric might have been totally turned off. So far, Christy hadn't said anything to him, either.

Sooner or later, he's going to find out, she told herself. *The later, the better,* she insisted silently. Right now, having Eric think she was just an ordinary girl felt good. Because that's exactly what she wanted to be. A regular, normal girl, not a sick one. Kara clung to the fantasy and hurried inside for her dreaded thumps.

Four

As Eric drove along aimlessly, he considered his good fortune. Ever since lunch, when Kara had come up to him, he'd been on a high. He recalled her in vivid detail and smiled. She was such a beautiful girl—blond with large brown eyes that totally dominated her elfin face. She was petite, like a little doll, even if she was a bit thin. But so what, he thought. Girls were always worrying about their weight. Even her voice intrigued him. It sounded breathy, slightly hoarse, and, he thought, sexy.

He couldn't wait to grill Christy about Kara. Maybe having Kara as a friend might take the edge of awkwardness off his relationship with his sister. It hadn't been easy for him to move in with her after almost six years, but then, anything beat living at home with parents who constantly hassled him.

Eric arrived at his sister's sprawling apartment complex and parked. He let himself in and wondered how the guys back home were doing and if they missed him. "Cool it," he told himself, forcing aside a wave of homesickness. He'd made his choice to move away, and he was sticking with it. He threw his books in the spare bedroom Christy had offered him for his own, wandered into the kitchen, stirred the contents of supper in the casserole and poured himself a bowl of cereal. He was sitting on the sofa, flipping through the TV channels, when Christy walked through the door. "No homework?" were the first words out of her mouth.

He flipped off the TV and slunk into the cushions. "I thought you weren't going to hassle me about school."

She dropped her car keys on the table and sighed. "You're right. I didn't mean to. Let's start over. How was your first day?"

"It was all right."

"You met Kara Fischer."

For the first time, he brightened. "I drove her home."

"I saw that." There was an edge to her tone that made him uneasy.

"I would have come and said hello, but she thought you didn't like people around when you worked." What Christy did professionally was very vague to him. He knew a physical therapist helped people recover from disabilities. One of his buddies back home had had a therapist help him after a football injury. For the first time all afternoon, he wondered why Christy worked with Kara. The pretty blond girl looked perfectly fine to him. More than fine.

"I'm glad the two of you met. She liked you."

The information pleased him. "She's one sweet babe," Eric said candidly. "A very sweet babe."

Christy had started for the kitchen, but turned on him the moment the comment was out of his mouth. "You be nice to her, Eric. She's not one of your silly bimbos."

Taken aback, Eric stared. "What are you talking about? 'My bimbos'?"

"Mom and Dad told me you were running with some pretty wild kids back home. They said some of your girlfriends weren't exactly high-quality. Kara's not that type."

Eric didn't try to hide his anger. "Mom and Dad had no right to talk about my friends that way. All Mom and Dad did was judge everybody."

"They said your friends were a bad influence on you. That sometimes you stayed out all night. They were worried sick about you. About what might happen to you if you remained in Houston."

"Look, when you said I could come live with you, I thought you weren't going to be my conscience. If I'd known I was trading one prison for another—"

"Please, I don't want to fight with you." Christy

held up her hand, and her voice softened. "I let you come live with me because I care about you, Eric. And believe it or not, so do Mom and Dad. We don't want to see you throw your life away. Life is very precious."

The seriousness of her expression made Eric feel baffled. "What's with you? I come home and tell you I really liked the girl *you* wanted me to meet, and you act as if I'm going to drag her off into the bushes."

"I did want the two of you to meet. But not for you to get ideas about dating her. I only wanted her to help you feel more comfortable making the transition to Central."

"Well, thanks for the vote of confidence about my morals, Christy." Eric's voice dripped with sarcasm. He sighed before adding, "Kara's a nice girl. I can tell that."

"Yes, she is. I like her a lot. I'm concerned for her—about her. Her life's not easy. She has CF."

"CF?" Eric followed Christy into the kitchen, where she began to take plates from the cupboards. "What's CF?"

"Cystic fibrosis."

"What's that?"

Christy turned and studied him. "You honestly don't know anything about what I do, do you?"

Eric rummaged through his limited knowledge about medicine. "Wait . . . I think I saw a telethon about CF once. Is it like asthma?"

Christy carefully set the plates onto the counter. "No. CF is a genetic disorder—you're born with it.

It's a disease of the exocrine glands. With CF, something goes wrong, and mucus turns thick and sticky. It jams up a person's lungs, sweat glands, and digestive tract."

Already Eric disliked the description. Who wanted to think about body fluids? "And Kara has this disease?"

"Don't worry. It isn't contagious."

"I didn't think it was," Eric insisted, although it wasn't true. He *had* wondered if he could catch it. Christy busied herself with setting the table. Eric dogged her steps into the dining room. "Is that all you're going to tell me about Kara? Is that why you give her therapy?"

"Yes. I administer her postural drainage therapy."

To Eric, the term sounded very technical, and he waved it aside. "So what's the big deal? She has therapy to help her breathe better. I don't see why that makes you so hyper. Is it because she's a patient and you have some kind of hangup about me dating one of your patients?"

Christy crossed her arms and once again turned to face him. "Eric, I don't think you truly understand the seriousness of Kara's illness."

"Is it incapacitating or something? She didn't look incapacitated to me."

"It hits some victims harder than others. Some people are plagued by lung and digestive disorders."

"So Kara's got it bad?"

"And there's something else about CF you should know."

"What's that?"

"There is no cure."

"So?" He swallowed, made suddenly uncomfortable by her blue-eyed gaze. "Aren't you helping her?"

"Not only is there no cure for CF," she said softly, ignoring his question, "it's fatal. One hundred percent fatal. Kara's just turned sixteen, but I doubt she'll live to celebrate her twentieth birthday."

Five

Kara poked at the food on her dinner plate. She tried to pretend she wanted it, mostly because her mother was watching like a hawk, but she wasn't the least bit hungry. She kept thinking about Eric and how wonderful she'd felt when she'd been with him.

"Did you take your enzyme pills?" her mother asked.

"Yes, Mom."

"Don't nag her, Renée," Kara's father interjected. "It's obvious she's not hungry."

Her mother ignored his reprimand. "Would you like me to fix you something else? I have a pizza in the freezer."

"No. The meat loaf's fine." Kara hoped she didn't sound as edgy as she felt. She knew her parents meant well, but it drove her crazy when they fussed over her and talked as if she weren't in the room. "You know that it takes a while for me to get my appetite back after a stint in the hospital."

"I still have some Vivonex," Mom said, naming the special food supplement that Kara sometimes drank in order to gain weight.

Kara grimaced. "I hate that stuff. Forget it. I'll get hungry again—stop worrying." She watched her parents exchange worried looks. "I'm *fine,*" Kara insisted, standing up. "Stop treating me like a baby." She tossed her napkin on the table. "I'll be in my room. I want to organize my notebook."

In her room, she flounced on the bed. The cheerful yellow and white walls and carpet seemed to mock her bad mood, and her bed, heaped with all sizes and shapes of pillows, suddenly felt like a cage. A soft rap on her door caused her to bury her face in her pile of pillows and shriek with pent-up frustration. She knew it was her mother coming to check up on her. "Yes?" Kara called.

Her mother opened the door and peeked inside the room. "Are you all right?"

"Mom, I'm fine. Sorry I snapped at you at the dinner table."

Her mother sat on the bed. "No . . . I'm the one who needs to apologize. I shouldn't have pressed you about supper. I worry about you, that's all." She smoothed Kara's hair, and Kara resisted the urge to pull away. "Your father and I don't mean to hound you—I've gotten better about not doing it, don't you think?"

Kara sat up and looked at her mother's anxious face. In many ways, she had gotten better, thanks to Vicki Diller, the psychologist Dr. McGee had insisted the family start seeing three years before. Before that, her mother had almost driven them all crazy trying to be responsible for Kara's illness. In fact, her overprotectiveness had almost caused her parents to divorce. At the therapist's suggestion, her mother was now working full-time. "Yes, you've gotten much better."

"Why don't you tell me about your first day of school?"

"Not much to tell. I want to stay well and have a good year."

"Is art still your favorite class?"

"Of course. I really want to go to art school after I graduate."

"Commercial artists make good money. Our agency is always looking for fresh talent."

"With a good job, I could get my own car and apartment." Kara began to warm up as she discussed her future.

She saw her mother's forehead pucker with concern, but heard her say, "Everyone needs their own space. Fortunately, you've got a few years before you need to think about that." Her mother *was* making an effort not to hover, and Kara felt grateful. "Any new faces at school this year?"

Kara casually mentioned Eric. "Any brother of Christy's must be a fine young man. I'd like to meet him."

Kara couldn't think of anything she'd rather *not* have happen. Both her parents would probably sit Eric down and grill him like a cheese sandwich. Her bedside phone rang, and she snatched it. "Where's the beautiful princess who's going to rescue me?" Vince asked, making Kara laugh.

"She's sitting on a mound of pillows, waiting for her own fairy godmother to make good on a few wishes. You've got a long wait."

"Just my luck." Vince paused. "How was day number one back at the salt mines of Central High?"

Kara mouthed Vince's name to her mother, who nodded, blew her a kiss, and left the room. "It's going to be a great year, Vince. How are you feeling? When will you be back?"

"Dr. McGee says the new antibiotic is doing the trick. I could be out in another week."

"That's super. Are you going stir-crazy yet?"

"Not as long as I've got the TV and my direct line to you."

She thought he sounded better, not as wheezy and certainly more upbeat. "I'll get by to see you this weekend."

"I'm looking forward to it. Tell me something exciting," Vince urged. "Nothing exciting is going on around here."

"Let's see . . . I met Christy's brother, Eric. He drove me home from school today."

"Tell me more."

"He comes from Texas and drives a fifty-seven Chevy that he seems to adore. Just my luck. A cute guy who's got a crush on a car." Vince grew quiet as she joked about Eric. "Of course, Eric doesn't know about my CF yet. I mean once he finds out, today may turn out to have been the *only* time I'll ride in his car." She laughed nervously.

"If it is, he's nuts."

"You're just saying that."

"No . . . but I'm hoping that he is nuts."

"You're silly." He coughed, and she clutched the receiver until he stopped. "You'd better get some rest."

"I'm tired of resting. I want to get out of this place."

"It won't be much longer."

"Sure." He sighed. "Well, my lovely, you take care. And remember, when the good fairy comes along, don't forget to include me in your wishes."

"Good-night, Vince," she said softly. "Thanks for calling."

"Good-night, princess. Don't forget me."

"Never." She hung up and stared at the receiver. Poor Vince. Still stuck in the hospital. This week, she was free of the place. Kara felt a tightness in her chest, making her realize that it was almost time for bed and that she needed her nightly thumps. Although she detested them, she went to the door to call her mother. She didn't want anything to get in the way of the plans she had for the new school term, which now included hope for a relationship with Eric Lawrence.

Six

Eric saw Kara coming down the crowded hallway between classes and ducked into the bathroom, hoping she hadn't seen him. A week had passed since Christy had told him about her condition, and for the life of him, he couldn't bring himself to want to be around Kara. The knowledge that she was sick enough to die totally repelled him. He'd tried to slough it off the afternoon Christy had first explained things to him. "Are you making that up?" he'd asked, knowing she wasn't, but hoping she was.

"Of course I'm not. Cystic fibrosis is incurable. Research has made life better than it used to be for its victims. Once, CFers didn't live beyond childhood. Now, some live into their mid-twenties, and those with less severe cases have lived to see their thirties."

"Don't they take medicine?" Eric wanted to know. "And what about all that therapy you do with Kara?"

"Yes, they take medicine, but the illness is still fatal. The therapy is important—it helps keep the mucus thinned and moving, but eventually, all victims fall prey to chronic lung diseases because germs and bacteria become trapped in the mucus. Lungs can collapse, they can begin to bleed, and eventually the heart may become enlarged and begin to fail. And many CFers have digestive disorders, as well."

Eric found Christy's knowledge impressive and thought that she really should have been a doctor. "Is that why Kara looks thin?" he asked.

Christy nodded. "Although she eats well, her food isn't absorbed properly, and that causes malnutrition."

Eric couldn't forget the dismay he'd felt as Christy explained the ramifications of living with CF. Every word of explanation felt like a blow, and by the time she'd listed all the complications and problems a CF victim encounters, all he wanted to do was forget about Kara Fischer altogether.

Except that he couldn't. No matter how hard he tried, he couldn't keep the image of her delicate, fragile face out of his mind. He couldn't forget the breathy quality of her voice, the eagerness of her smile, the play of sunlight in her golden hair.

She didn't deserve to have something like cystic fibrosis. Why was life so unfair?

From the first time he'd set eyes on Kara, he'd felt drawn to her. She'd had a quality about her that said "special," just as surely as if a sign had been hung around her neck. While he would have never admitted it to his sister, the girls he had dated in Houston weren't go great, and he'd figured that in Kara, he'd found all the right qualities. But now, knowing about her CF—well, what kind of future was there in dating her?

He purposely decided to avoid her. If he ran into her in the halls, he waved, but kept moving. If he saw her in the cafeteria, he made it a point to sit with some of the guys. Now, seeing her heading straight toward him in the hallway had forced him into the bathroom. "Chicken," he muttered under his breath, feeling ashamed of not being able to deal with her.

Eric splashed cold water on his face. He came up sputtering and heard a guy say, "Hey, man."

Eric recognized him from his English class. "What?"

"Did you do the English assignment? I didn't. Could you share?"

Eric actually had done the assignment. He didn't like people who cheated. He knew he should tell the guy to buzz off, but without thinking, he answered, "Naw. I didn't do it, either."

The boy swore. "It's a stupid class, anyway. Maybe I won't go."

"Suit yourself."

"Say, why don't you come with me? I'll show you a hot spot much more interesting than this dump."

Eric considered the offer. He knew he shouldn't cut class. What if Christy found out? But he knew he didn't want to be around school, either. What if he ran into Kara again? Seeing her in the halls made him think about things he didn't want to think about. "I guess I could," he said.

"Great. Just as soon as the bell rings, I'll check the halls, and if they're clear, we're out of here."

Minutes later, the two of them made a dash to the parking lot.

Kara had seen Eric in the crush of people changing classes, and her heart had done a flip-flop. She started to call his name, but saw him go into the bathroom, and her greeting died on her lips. A hot flush spread up her neck and face. There was no longer any doubt in her mind—Eric Lawrence was avoiding her on purpose. She replayed the afternoon they'd spent together for the thousandth time. Again, she felt the wind in her hair as she rode in his car, smelled the scent of the car's cracked leather seats, heard the songs that had played on the radio. What had she done wrong? Had she said something to turn him off?

"You'd better start moving, or you'll get run over," Elyse kidded, coming up alongside her.

Kara started. "Sorry. I was daydreaming. Temporary insanity." Kara started walking, and Elyse rushed to keep up.

"You've been preoccupied all week. What gives?"

Kara hadn't been able to confide in Elyse, her mother, or Christy about her feelings concerning Eric. His rejection of her stung. "I'm just busy getting settled into the routine. Mr. Carney wants me to enter something into the all-state art competition. I've been considering what to draw," she said breezily.

The crowd in the halls had thinned, and Kara neared the art room. "Have you seen Eric today?" Elyse asked. "I thought you two might become an item after your fantastic first encounter."

Kara tried to keep her face expressionless. "Nothing's happening with us. I told you, I was only doing Christy a favor."

"I saw Sheila Morrison hanging all over him yesterday." Elyse rolled her eyes to make her point. "That girl is *so* tacky."

Kara had heard stories about Sheila, but Elyse's nasty attitude made her angry. She knew how it felt to have people whisper behind her back. Whenever kids learned about her illness, they talked about it with other students, but never to her outright. "Elyse, it's a free world. If Eric wants to hang with Sheila, I could care less."

"You don't have to bite my head off. I was only telling you what I saw."

Kara wished she could level with her friend and tell her how she really felt, but remembering how Elyse had reacted to the spring dance business with Kevin, she didn't want to risk any of Elyse's speculations. "I'm going to be late for class."

"Will you call me later?" Elyse asked.

She turned toward Elyse, who stood in the hall, looking dejected. "Of course, but please stop talking about Eric around me, all right?"

Without waiting for Elyse to answer, Kara hurried into the art room and then slunk to the back of the room, where she succumbed to a fit of coughing.

By the time Kara arrived home from school, her chest felt tight and her head feverish. As she rummaged in the medicine chest for medicine, she fought down a sense of panic. She couldn't get sick again. She just couldn't. She'd barely gotten out of the hospital. Kara washed two tablets down with water as she heard the doorbell. She quickly dabbed cover cream on the dark circles under her eyes, ran a brush through her hair, hurried to the front door, and let Christy in.

"I thought you'd stood me up," Christy said with a smile.

"That's not my style," Kara countered, all the while thinking, *Like your brother's.*

They went into Kara's sunny bedroom and started the procedure, but all Kara could think of was Eric and how he was snubbing her. Once the therapy was over and she'd coughed until she was hoarse, they went into the kitchen. Kara fixed glasses of iced tea for them.

The medicine had done its work, and she was

feeling less feverish. "How's your brother liking Central?" she asked as casually as possible.

"He says it's all right. But surely he's told you how he likes it by now."

" 'Fraid not. He hardly speaks to me at school."

Christy set her glass of tea on the counter, a look of guilt crossing her pretty face. "I'm sorry."

Kara saw the look. "You told him about my CF, didn't you?"

"He asked me."

"He didn't know to ask. I never said a word to him."

"Oh, Kara, I didn't mean any harm, but I was concerned for you."

"For me? Why? I liked him. And he seemed to like me. At least, before he knew. I thought we were friends, Christy."

Christy looked stricken. "We *are* friends. That's why the truth is so important. I don't want anyone to hurt you, even my brother—especially my brother."

"I don't have enough problems with my parents?" Kara slid off the kitchen stool and began pacing.

"I didn't mean to meddle."

"Don't you think I wonder what it would be like to have a regular guy notice me? Don't you think I want to be accepted as—as a girl with normal feelings? Do you have any idea what it's like to feel as if every breath I take in mixed company is some kind of a turnoff?"

Christy reached out to touch Kara's arm."Wait a minute. Please. Of course, I understand that you want to be accepted. Why, only a complete idiot wouldn't accept you."

Kara recalled how the boys at school treated her—friendly, but strictly hands-off. "Then the world is full of idiots."

"Frankly, most teenage guys just aren't equipped emotionally to handle a meaningful relationship."

"You mean Eric?"

Kara saw color creep up Christy's cheeks. "Eric's my brother, and I love him, but he's not the boy for you, Kara. He's got plenty of problems of his own."

"He doesn't have CF."

"Touché." Christy sighed. "I'll speak to him."

"Don't you dare!" Christy's remark galvanized Kara into action. "If you say even one word about this talk we've had, I'll never forgive you."

"All right. Calm down. I'll stay out of it. Promise." She crossed her heart.

Once Christy had gone, Kara sat in bed with her drawing pad, unable to put Eric out of her mind. Christy had said he had problems. Kara should have asked for details. What problems could a sixteen-year-old as good-looking as Eric Lawrence possibly have? She gave a mirthless laugh. "He'll never get close enough for me to know."

She sketched randomly until her room grew deep with shadows. She didn't like any of her artwork, and in exasperation, she tossed the pad aside. The doorbell rang, startling her. She shimmied off the bed, and when she opened the door, she was greeted by Vince Chapman. "Hi, beautiful," he said, flipping the ends of her hair with his fingers.

Seven

"VINCE!" KARA SQUEALED, throwing her arms around his neck. "When did they cut you loose?"

"This afternoon," he said with a laugh. "I went home, but then headed right over here."

"You didn't tell me."

"I wanted to surprise you."

She unwrapped her arms from his neck and dragged him inside. "You should have said something."

"And missed out on this greeting? No way." He followed her into her living room. "Did your folks forget to pay their electric bill?"

Kara realized that she'd not turned on any lights and flipped on switches. "Dad's flying an overnighter, and Mom had some big agency planning meeting. I hadn't realized it was so late."

"Have you eaten?"

"I forgot to." Kara chewed on her lip. "Mom'll kill me. She made up this tray of food I was supposed to pop into the microwave for my dinner."

"Still no appetite?"

"Not a bit," Kara admitted, although she now wondered how much of its loss was due to Eric's lack of interest.

"I'm having trouble getting mine back, too," Vince admitted. "Maybe between us we can polish off that stuff your mother fixed."

"It's a deal." Kara led Vince into the kitchen and parked him at the counter while she found the tray in the fridge. As it warmed in the microwave, she set plates and silver on the counter. Vince sat on a stool, observing. "So, when will you be back at school?" she asked.

"Monday. I've been keeping up with the assignments, but socially, I'll be my usual outcast self. How's it going between you and Christy's brother?"

Vince's question sounded casual, but Kara knew she sounded curt when she answered. "First Elyse, now you. For heaven's sake, I barely know the guy. What's all this interest in my nonrelationship with Eric?"

"I'm interested in everything you're interested in," Vince said. His dark eyes regarded her expectantly. "Old habit, I guess. I've never had that many friends."

Kara felt bad about snapping at him. "Okay, so we've never been part of the in crowd. But that doesn't mean we can't keep trying to expand our circle."

"This is my senior year. If I haven't expanded my circle by now, I doubt I will."

"Will you graduate in June?"

"Too soon to tell. I hope so, but I'm behind in everything."

"If you do, then what?"

"Community college. And a job. If I can hold one. I wish I could plan for something more exciting."

She understood—plans for the future hinged on staying well.

His gaze lingered on her face. "I've got to get through Christmas first."

Haven't we both, she thought, but didn't say it. The microwave beeped, and Kara removed the tray and divided the food.

"Smells good," Vince said, reaching into his pocket for his enzyme medication.

Kara swallowed her pills also. "Mom's a good cook. What a shame it's wasted on me." He ate and declared it delicious. "The student council's sponsoring a carnival for Halloween," she mentioned between bites. "There'll be booths, a flea market, and a haunted house. They're busing in some inner-city kids."

"Sort of like the white suburbs does its conscience bit for the community?"

"Don't be sarcastic. It'll be fun."

"What'll you be doing for the cause?"

"I'm in the face painting booth."

"Will you paint my face?"

"Sure . . . for three dollars."

"I thought you said this was for poor kids."

She giggled at his attempt to sound miserly. "It's only free to kids under age ten. Big people have to pay."

"Maybe I can get back into the swing of things at school if I volunteer to do something," Vince said thoughtfully. "You say there'll be a haunted house?"

"That's right. I volunteered to work on the planning committee, and I could get you into it. What would you like to do?"

"I could come as Count Dracula, since I look sort of ghoulish."

"You look fine, but if you want to be the count, I'll do your makeup," she offered.

"A deal I can't refuse. Of course, I couldn't refuse anything you offered me."

She smiled. "You're a good friend, Vince. I'm glad we have each other."

He looked at her across the table, and his expression grew serious. "Me, too. I've felt that way for years, you know—glad that you were in my life."

She was at a momentary loss for words. She liked Vince. He was a part of her life. But even now, looking straight at him, she felt the image of Eric nudge into her brain. "All right then. Let me set you up with the kids doing the haunted house," Kara said quickly, returning to their former topic of conversation. "I'm sure they'll be glad to have you on their team."

He rose from the stool, gave an elaborate bow, and kissed the back of her hand. "The count must leave you now, my dear." He mimicked the accent of Hollywood's best vampires.

She walked him to the door and watched him drive off into the night. Life was full of tricks. Vince was the original Mr. Nice Guy, and she really valued their relationship. But Eric—Eric was tall, muscled, witty, handsome. He was the one she longed to be with. He was the one she wanted, but he didn't seem to want her.

Eric was lying on his bed, skimming the text of a Shakespearean play, his headphones clamped to his head, the sound of music blaring against his eardrums. He was startled to glance up and see his sister standing at the foot of his bed. He tugged off the headset and poked the switch on his cassette player. "Hey, sis. What's up? I didn't hear you knock."

"We need to talk."

Christy wasn't smiling, and Eric knew immediately that she was about to launch into a lecture. He sighed, sat upright. "So, talk."

"Did you skip school last week?" He avoided her direct gaze. "Don't lie to me, Eric."

"Is that what you think I'm going to do? Lie about it?" Anger edged his voice.

"I know you cut your afternoon classes," she

said without answering his question. "I want to know why."

He pressed his lips together tightly. "No reason. Sorry."

"Eric, you promised that if I let you come live with me, you'd abide by my terms—which weren't unreasonable. And the terms were *no* cutting classes. School's important. I only wish I were still in school. Anyway, skipping out during classes isn't acceptable."

"No wild partying. No breaking curfew. No running with the wrong crowd," he added in a singsong as he stood up. "I remember all the rules. There're too many rules."

Christy snapped, "You agreed to them."

"I know." Silence fell between them, and Eric rocked back on his heels.

"Why do you do it?" Christy asked. "Why do you purposely go out of your way to get in trouble?"

"You sound like our parents." His tone was sarcastic.

"Mom and Dad are good parents. They help us as best they can. I know they want a good life for you."

At that, Eric shoved clenched hands into the pockets of his jeans. "I know what they want. Why doesn't anybody bother with what I want?"

"Maybe you could be more specific. What do you want?"

"I guess I want to be my own person."

"That doesn't mean anything to me. What do

you want to do with your life? Life's not just fun and games, you know."

He threw up his hands in frustration. "I don't know what I want to *be.* I only know I don't want what Dad wants for me. I don't want to take over his stupid hardware store. I don't want to be the dutiful son, smiling at all his customers, making small talk with 'good old boys' and sorting through bins of bolts for just the right one to fix some guy's dumb lawn mower."

"Do you want to go to college?"

"I don't know."

"You're smart enough."

"I'm not nuts about hitting the books, and I wouldn't know what to study if I went."

"You like your car. If you study hard, maybe you can be an engineer or even a car designer."

"Yes, I like my car. I like tinkering under the hood and making the engine purr. I like to take cars apart and put them back together again."

"You *feel* things deeply," Christy insisted. "You need to deal with your feelings and set some goals."

He averted his eyes. He didn't like people knowing that much about him, even his sister. Eric hated feeling vulnerable. It seemed to be a sign of weakness. It was easy for him to deal with machines. Machines had no feelings and no expectations. "I'm sorry I skipped school," he said dully. "I won't do it again."

Christy came a few steps closer. "Eric, I remember what it was like to be sixteen. The ups and downs of it. All I can tell you is that you'll live through it." He hated her sermon, but kept his thoughts to himself. "Life isn't perfect, and we all have disappointments. You're my brother, and I understand that you might not be able to fit into Dad's mold. We all want what's best for you. We may not know what that is, but then, neither do you."

"I get your point," he replied.

Christy looked him in the eye. "Eric, we're all trying to help you. My job is demanding and full of stress. My responsibilities to my patients are a priority. I can't be worried about them and you, too. They can't help their condition. You can. Something must remain constant in my life if I'm going to help all the people who count on me."

Like Kara Fischer, he thought, shocked by the instant, vivid picture of her that rose in his mind. "I said I get the point."

"Eric, I love you, but I can't have a wild hare on my hands. Please keep your promises to me about house and school rules. Don't blow it again, or I'll send you straight back to Houston. And until you're eighteen, that's where you'll have to stay."

He met the challenge in her eyes. He knew she wasn't bluffing. He didn't want to go back, but at that moment he didn't want to stay, either. He felt as if he had no choices. Go back and face conforming to his father's image. Stay and drown in Christy's rules. Eric nodded slowly. "I won't let you down again. I'll be on my best behavior for the rest of the school year."

"I'll take you at your word," she said, then left the room.

He stared at the doorway for a long time, his insides a jumble. He would make it through the school year. But come summer, he would pack up and leave. And not for Houston, either. Come summer, he would hit the road, and none of his family would have to see his face, or hassle him, ever again.

Eight

ERIC NOTICED A tall, extremely thin guy with dark hair weave his way between the rows of desks of the English class. The boy greeted kids who seemed to know him.

"Hey, Vince," Eric heard Sheila say as he passed by her desk.

"Hey, yourself," Vince answered, and when he smiled, Eric saw white, straight teeth, and decided that some girls might think the guy good-looking.

"Who's he?" Eric whispered to Sheila after Vince had taken a seat in the back of the room.

She wrote "Vince Chapman" on a piece of notebook paper and shoved it toward Eric. The name meant nothing to Eric. Still, he wondered why Vince was starting classes so late in the term. Before he could find out more from Sheila, the teacher broke the class into groups to work on performing a scene from a Shakespearean play. Eric found himself in a group of six with Vince.

Howie was talking to Vince, and Eric pretended he wasn't listening in on them. "I thought you were a senior, Vince. How'd you'd get stuck back here with us junior lowlifes?"

"I had to take double English credits," Vince explained, "since I missed too many classes last year."

Howie made a face. "Bummer."

"It's not so bad. I don't have to take phys ed, so I've got the time for extra English."

Eric thought, *You could use phys ed, buddy.*

"So, how're things going for you?" Howie asked. "You know—the hospital and all."

"I'm on what I call 'leave.' I never count myself as totally out," Vince said, and turned toward Eric. "I know the others here, but you're new to me."

Eric grunted his name and added, "I just transferred from Houston this year."

"I think we have a mutual friend—Kara Fischer."

Eric shook Vince's extended hand. "Right. I know Kara," Eric said, suddenly uncomfortable under Vince's piercing gaze.

"Kara's told me about you," Vince offered.

Eric shrugged. "I don't know her too well."

"I do," Vince stated. "She's one of my best friends."

When Eric looked into Vince's eyes, he thought

he saw some kind of a challenge. He bristled. Was this lightweight telling him that Kara was his territory? "I have lots of friends," Eric said carefully. "It's a big school."

Sheila leaned over and said, "I'll be your friend, Eric."

The others laughed, and Eric smiled good-naturedly. "I always have time for a pretty girl."

Vince met Eric's gaze steadily. "Time's a funny thing. Sometimes it runs out on you."

In a sudden flash of understanding, Eric realized that Vince had CF, too. The discussion about the hospital had been a clue, and his thin body and clubbed fingers were obvious signs. Eric felt ashamed of coming on so tough, but didn't know how to back down. Howie relieved the tension. "Hey, guys, can we get on with this play? We're getting dirty looks from you know who already."

Eric quickly picked up his book. He didn't want to memorize a scene from some tragedy about life and death. He wanted to leave the room, go outside into the sunshine, and blow off some steam. He wanted to forget about Vince and Kara and their being sick. Life sure could be unfair.

After school, Eric hurried through the halls, trying to avoid people. He rounded a corner and stopped abruptly. Kara was standing in front of a bank of lockers, talking to Vince. She was looking up at him while he leaned down protectively over her. As she laughed, Eric heard the distant sound of her voice.

Eric wondered what Vince was saying that she

found so funny. She had laughed that way for him the day he'd driven her home. Of course, then he hadn't known that she was sick. And now that he did—well, he wished he felt different about it, but he didn't. Yet, it definitely bothered him to see her and Vince together.

He flung open his locker. The metal door hit the wall with a bang. If he didn't care, why was it bugging him? He couldn't understand his reaction. He couldn't understand a lot of things lately. Like why it had mattered to him when Vince had told him that Kara was so close, they were best friends. He marched out to the parking lot, jumped into his car, turned his radio up full blast, and drove out of the parking lot with a squeal of tires.

The Saturday before Halloween, Elyse came over to Kara's house. "I'm not sure what to wear to the carnival while I paint faces," Kara told her.

"I'm going as Little Bo Peep," Elyse said, flopping onto Kara's bed. "I'm supposed to guide groups of kids through the haunted house—the really young ones. The teacher in charge thought it would seem less scary if the guides dressed like friendly types from Mother Goose. I'd prefer to go as a vampire or something sexy or elegant. I'm fed up with this plain Jane me."

Kara held up a black body stocking. "I had Mom buy this for me. I thought I'd go as a black cat. But now I'm not sure I should wear it."

"Why not? Let me see."

Kara pulled on the body suit she'd transformed into her costume. There was a black hood on which she'd sewn pointed ears, and on the back, she'd attached a long tail she'd made out of black velvet. "I thought I could paint whiskers on my face, do my eyes dark and dramatic, and decorate the backs of my hands with tufts of velvet and black nail polish."

"Wow, you look terrific," Elyse exclaimed.

"Do you think so?" Kara studied herself in the mirror hanging on the inside of her closet door. The body suit clung tight, making her look sleek and taut. She put her hand near her face, cupped like a cat's paw, and purred, then burst out laughing.

"I sure do," Elyse declared. "One ounce of fat, and you couldn't wear that thing."

"Fat's not a problem."

"Are you going to Howie's party afterward?"

"Yes. Vince wants to take me. I guess you're still grounded. I wish your parents would let you go."

"I'm grounded like a pumpkin in a pumpkin patch. I even cried, but Mom wouldn't budge. She said I should be glad I can be Little Bo Peep." She picked at the bedspread. "You're sure seeing a lot of Vince. Are you guys getting serious?"

"You know we're just friends."

"Maybe—just *maybe*—Vince doesn't think so."

"I like Vince a lot, but only as a friend. And he likes me as a friend, too. He's just fixated on me right now because he's been in the hospital and I understand about CF. There's no one else except his family who understands."

Elyse looked ashamed. "I should have visited him in the hospital. I meant to. He's a really nice guy."

Kara almost told her that good intentions didn't count for much when a person was lying alone and forgotten in the hospital. She said nothing, knowing it would only make Elyse feel worse and put a damper on the afternoon.

Elyse picked up Kara's sketch pad and started flipping through it. "Hey, these are good. I recognize none other than Eric Lawrence."

Feeling her cheeks color, Kara crossed the room and tugged the pad from Elyse's hands. "It's just old stuff," she said. "He's got an interesting face—plenty of planes and angles. I thought I'd try and draw his face from memory. It's good practice."

Elyse turned a few pages of the pad. "Well, you've done a great job. It really looks like him. I guess you would have told me if he'd given you another ride home?"

"Yes, I would have, but he hasn't." Kara stared down at the various pencil drawings of Eric's brooding good looks. She knew that the drawings were good. She'd been working on capturing her friends—she wished she didn't feel so connected to a guy who didn't care. She'd captured something she'd felt when she'd been with him—something he'd tried to hide—his vulnerability. She slapped the pad shut and shoved it in a drawer. "You know I sketch people all the time.

Anyway, the only thing Christy's ever said is that Eric's busy with school."

"What do you think about Eric and Vince's having a class together?"

The news surprised her. "I think Vince may have mentioned that," she said without meeting Elyse's eyes. She knew he hadn't, and the fact that he hadn't bothered her. Why wouldn't he have said something?

"I hear girls talking about Eric," Elyse added. "The story is he's really good-looking, but fickle. He dates someone a few times, then drops her, without giving her a clue as to why."

"What are you—a field reporter for *The Nashville Banner*?"

"I was just telling you what I've heard," Elyse answered. "I just thought you'd like to know."

"Well, I don't. What Eric Lawrence does and who he sees isn't the least bit interesting to me." But even as she said the words, Kara knew she was lying. It *did* matter to her what Eric did. It mattered a whole lot. Even though she wished with all her heart that it didn't.

Nine

"Do you think you should go?"

Kara heard the anxious tone of her mother's question and purposely ignored it. "Of course. I've been planning for this, and besides, everybody's counting on me."

"But your cough—"

"I'm fine, Mom. I'm not coughing now at all." Kara knew her mother was right. She shouldn't go, but she refused to give in. She'd taken medicine and plenty of cough syrup with codeine all afternoon. Her chest felt tight, and it was hard to catch her breath as she dressed, but she was determined not to stay home. *Please, God, don't let me get sick tonight,* she prayed silently. More than anything, she wanted to go to the carnival and the party.

"You'll have Vince bring you home if you feel worse, won't you?" her mother insisted.

"You know I will." The doorbell rang. "That's Vince now. Bring him back here so I can start on his makeup."

"Kara, I—"

"Mom, please . . ." She turned pleading eyes toward her mother. "It's just one night. One time for fun. Don't I deserve one normal night? I'll be all right."

Her mother left and returned with Vince, smiling and asking him questions. Kara felt a flood of gratitude toward her mother for acting as if everything were normal. Once he was seated at Kara's vanity, she left them alone.

"Are you wearing your bathrobe to the carnival?" Vince teased.

"There's a cat suit under it," she said. "Do you like my makeup?"

"It looks great." He leaned closer. "I like your whiskers and your button nose."

"Sit still or I'll draw your eyebrows on crooked."

He caught her wrist and searched her face with his gaze. "You're not well, are you? I can hear it."

She saw no reason to lie to Vince. "I started running a tiny fever this morning, and I'm coughing. But I've been pumping cough syrup with codeine, and I feel pretty good right now."

"I'll bet," Vince said dryly. "You know we don't have to go. I don't mind staying here with you."

"I'm not staying home," she said stubbornly.

"Listen, I want to take you to that party as much as you want to go."

"But you'll understand if I have to leave early?"

"Just say the word, and I'll have you out of there faster than a bat out of—"

She put her fingers against his lips. "Don't say it."

He grinned, then grew serious and stroked the side of her cheek with the back of his hand. "I'll take care of you, Kara. For just as long as you need me, I'll take care of you."

The school halls were swarming with kids of all sizes in every manner of costume by the time Kara and Vince arrived. Smells of chalk and library paste had been replaced by scents of popcorn, caramel apples, and cotton candy. The gym had been turned into a haunted house, where screams and bloodcurdling cackles rose from audio tapes as well as from people touring.

As Vince and Kara approached the darkened room, small children moved aside, eyes growing wide at the sight of Vince's sweeping black cape and vampire teeth. He hissed at one small boy, who ducked behind an older one. Kara whispered, "Sorry I made us late."

"No problem. Where're you headed?"

"My booth's set up in the cafeteria."

"Do you want a tour of the haunted house before you go?"

"No, thanks. I never did like the dark."

He took her hand. "I'll come get you as soon as

we close up shop here, then we'll go to the party if you're up to it."

"I'll be up to it." She was feeling better. A bit numb and lightheaded, but at least she didn't have a constant urge to cough. "See you," she told him, and walked to the cafeteria, touching the wall for support because her knees felt rubbery.

Once inside, she wove through droves of children and stalls, games and vendors until she found the art booth. "It's about time," one of the senior girls snapped. "You were supposed to be here half an hour ago."

"Sorry. My date had car trouble." She didn't like lying, but she couldn't say she was sick, either.

"Well, get busy," the girl ordered. "There's a line a mile long."

Kara set to work at once on a small girl dressed as a fairy princess who wanted a butterfly on her cheek. Kara's hands trembled when she picked up a paintbrush. She fought to control them. *You can do this,* she told herself, and before long, Kara settled into a rhythm. Soon she lost count of all the faces she painted. And even though her back and arms ached, she was having a good time.

"Can you paint dragons?" a male voice asked.

Kara paused from cleaning her brush and stared up at Eric Lawrence. A flood of emotions swept through her. She wanted to act cool and distant toward him. She wanted to smile and flirt with him. "If that's what you want," she ended up saying, rather stiffly, "a dragon you'll get."

He sat in the metal chair in front of her. His

shoulders were broad, his chest wide, making her feel small, like a bedraggled kitten. His brown hair swept over his forehead, and his eyelashes, long and thick, intensified the aqua blue of his eyes. He regarded her through half-closed lids.

She dabbed her brush into a pot of green paint. "You want a cartoon dragon or the real thing?"

"The real thing, of course."

She began to create a dragon's face with the brush and saw him smile. "What's wrong?"

"It tickles."

"It won't take long."

"Don't hurry."

She felt her heart hammer against her rib cage and wondered if it was the effects of her medications or his nearness. "Do you want the dragon breathing fire?"

"What do you think?"

"I would guess you do." She swirled red-yellow flames from the dragon's mouth. She was so close to him that she caught the scent of his breath—cool and minty. When she finished, she backed away and surveyed her handiwork. She thought it pretty good. "All done," she told Eric, as business-like as possible.

He was staring at her hands, at her funny-looking clubbed fingers. She quickly put the brush aside and slipped them under the smock she was wearing over her costume.

Eric glanced into a hand mirror alongside her brushes. "You do good work. Thanks." He stood, looking down at her, and for a moment, she thought he might say something else. But he didn't, and she watched him walk away. Why did he always make her feel as if she were on a roller coaster? She hated the constant turmoil she felt every time she was around him, but couldn't bear the thought of not feeling it, either. *Face it,* she told herself angrily, *you're going crazy, and all because of Eric Lawrence.*

By the time the carnival wound down, Kara had painted over fifty faces. She was exhausted. She'd been fighting off a constant urge to cough. Her chest felt as if bands of steel were tightening around it, her head hurt. She knew her fever was rising. She slipped into the bathroom, took more cough syrup, and rested her cheek against the cool tile. "Give it up, body," she muttered through gritted teeth. "I'm *going* to that party."

By the time Vince came for her, she was feeling more human. They drove to Howie's, a large Colonial-style house right outside the city, on rolling pasture land. They parked alongside a white split-rail fence and walked up a shale driveway slowly, so that Kara could catch her breath. A full harvest moon shone down in a clear, star-studded sky, and an autumn chill tinged the air. The cold felt good to Kara, and she almost hated going inside the house filled with noise and light and too many dancing kids.

People called greetings, but all Kara wanted to do was find a chair and regain her strength. "Let me get you something to drink," Vince shouted above the music and voices as he deposited her on a sofa.

Too out of breath to speak, she gave him a thumbs-up signal. Her lungs felt on fire. She longed to cough, but held her breath until the urge passed. She watched Vince shoulder his way back through the crowd, balancing two sodas. He sat on the arm of the sofa beside her, putting his free arm around her protectively. "You sure you're all right?"

She took a big swig of the cola. "No problem." She wanted to change the subject. "Everybody looks great," she told him.

Around them, people in colorful costumes danced. "You're the only black cat," Vince said, leaning down toward her ear. "And a beautiful cat, too. Pur-r-rfect, I'd say."

"You big bloodsucker . . . I'll bet you say that to all the girls."

Vince laughed. "Howie has a basement full of video games. Will you come with me downstairs and we can try a few?"

Kara didn't want to navigate the stairs, or manipulate the buttons for the games. "Go on without me," she urged. "I'd just like to sit here a while and watch everybody. I'm okay. Don't treat me like I'm sick, Vince. Please."

"You sure?"

She gave him a little shove. "Go on."

Vince bent and kissed her forehead. "I won't be gone long." He untied his black cape and laid it across her lap. "I don't want this thing in my way.

'Vait for me.' " He used his best Transylvanian accent.

"I 'vill,' " she mimicked. The urge to cough was overwhelming her. She remembered how cool the night air had felt and decided she needed to get outside before she fainted.

Kara threaded her way through the throngs of dancers and was almost to the doorway when an arm reached out and circled her waist. "Look what I caught," a familiar voice said.

She felt herself spun around, locked in a muscled embrace. As she came to a stop, she looked up to see a fire-breathing dragon staring down.

Ten

"Dance with me?" Eric asked. Someone had lowered the lights, and a slow song was playing.

Before Kara could say anything, he locked his arms around her and began moving with the music. Eric's arms felt solid and secure, and the flannel of his shirt felt soft against her cheek. She felt as if she were floating. Her heart hammered, then slowed as she lost herself in the music and the sheer physical nearness of him. "Everybody's telling me that the dragon you painted is awesome," he reported.

She pulled back only slightly. "What is your costume, anyway?"

He was dressed in jeans, boots, and a shirt with one sleeve torn off so that his large biceps showed. A bandanna was wound around his forehead. "Texas barroom brawler."

"You fit the role." She snuggled back into his chest.

"And you fit pretty good right here."

All too soon for Kara, the song ended, and breathless, she drew away. Adrenaline had carried her through the dance, but now her physical strength started to ebb. Silently, she cursed her weak lungs, her lousy genetics. "I was headed out for fresh air," she told him as casually as she could.

"I'll come with you." He held her hand and led the way outdoors. She followed him along a flagstone patio, down a terraced pathway, toward a single pine tree that kept a lone vigil alongside the split-rail fence. Moonlight spilled across rolling meadows and gave the night a ghostly quality.

Kara used the tree's trunk for support, and discreetly turned her head and coughed, clearing her lungs as quietly as possible, ignoring the cough's attempt to rip out of her. The chilly night air permeated her flimsy cat suit, and she struggled to keep her teeth from chattering. She couldn't bear the thought of deserting this moment in the moonlight with Eric just because she was cold.

"You're freezing," he observed, rubbing her arms briskly with his hands.

"Just a little."

"Put this on." He took Vince's cape, which was still draped over her arm, and which she'd all but forgotten while they'd danced, and draped it over her shoulders. It offered surprising warmth. He tied it under her chin. She didn't trust herself to look up into his eyes, because then he'd know—really know—how she felt about him.

"There," he said, his big fingers fumbling with a lopsided bow. He stepped back and leaned on the split-rail fence.

"Thanks," she said. She studied him. Why couldn't he simply act flip and clever, as he had the first day they'd met? She wished she could turn back the clock and relive the lightheartedness of that afternoon, before he'd known about her CF.

"What am I going to do about you, Kara?"

His tone was subdued and so sincere that his question caught her by surprise. "What do you mean?"

"I can't stay away from you."

"You seem to be doing a fine job of it," she said quietly, but without malice.

"I know it seems that way, but you don't know how hard it's been."

She was skeptical. "We just danced together, but after tonight, how will it be between us? Will you still ignore me in the halls? Will you duck into the nearest open door whenever you see me coming?"

He turned his head, and she saw his jaw clench. She thought he might walk away, but instead he asked, "What's between you and Vince?"

"We're friends."

"Vince doesn't act as if he's just your friend."

"Vince understands me. We're a lot alike." There were so many things she couldn't say to Eric because she didn't want him to think of her as sick.

"I would like to understand you, too." Eric's words came haltingly.

No you wouldn't, she thought, knowing the overwhelming burden of her illness. He had no idea what he was asking. "Haven't you ever had a best friend?"

"No. I've only had lots of friends. Tons of friends," Eric added sardonically. "I've always known how to have a good time, and people like me for that."

Especially the girls, she thought. "Having fun's important."

"I don't get close to people very often. It keeps things from getting complicated. But with you and Vince—it's different. I can tell."

"Vince and I go back a long time. We've always shared this condition." She hated to bring up her illness. "People who aren't sick don't understand. Christy does. It's complicated." She shrugged and stared up at him. "What do you want me to be to you?" She wasn't sure where she found the boldness to ask such a question, but she had to know. She didn't want to be one of "Eric's girls."

"I'm still trying to figure it out." Her heart sank. What had she expected? A pledge of commitment and devotion? She turned her head, and Eric quickly added, "I didn't mean that the way it came out. I guess I want to get to know you better. It's a start."

Knowing her meant knowing about CF. And accepting it. "I'd like that," she blurted out before she could stop her lips from saying what her heart was feeling.

"And Vince?"

"He and I will always have a special relationship. Why does it have to be either-or? It's different with both of you."

"It usually doesn't work out for a girl to bounce between two guys."

She wanted to debate with him, but her chest was tightening up again and a headache pounded behind her eyes. She was certain that her fever had returned.

"Kara?" Vince's voice called to her, and she and Eric both turned toward it. Vince was standing in the moonlight, in his costume. He looked like a prince out of darkness from a fairy tale. For Kara, his presence was like a lifeline thrown to a drowning person. She was sick, and he would help her. She trusted him.

"I'm here," she said.

Vince ignored Eric, came up beside her, and put his arm around her. Gratefully, she leaned into him, and immediately, he bolstered her with his body. "I was thinking that I should get you home," Vince said, sounding casual. "You know what happens to us vampires if the rays of the sun hit us."

Kara's knees felt rubbery, and if it hadn't been

for Vince's arms, they would have buckled. Inwardly, she pleaded, *Don't let Eric see me get sick.* "I wouldn't want to be responsible for your turning to dust particles," she managed as cheerfully as she could.

Vince turned to Eric. "So, we're splitting. See you at school next week."

Scowling, Eric shoved his hands into the hip pockets of his jeans. "Sure. I'll see you Monday," he said directly to Kara.

"We've got that scene to read in English," Vince said. "Do you know your lines?"

"Like my own name."

Kara wasn't sure she could stand upright, even with Vince's help. Deftly he led her around the back of the house, and as soon as they were out of sight of the pine tree, he scooped her up into his arms and carried her.

"I can walk," she mumbled against his neck.

"You can't even stand," he said, his own breath coming hard.

"But you'll have problems. Your lungs—"

"Hush. Don't make it any worse. I want to be able to help you. To be strong for you." He didn't say "like Eric," but she knew what he was thinking. Pain racked her, and breathing became more difficult. "It's not much farther," he said.

In a daze, she watched the house recede in the distance, watched the moonlight falling like a pale white shroud, and saw in her mind's eye Eric standing against the fence, his arms crossed, while the dragon on his cheek spit fire.

* * *

Kara lay in her bed, propped up with pillows, her breath coming in short, rapid gasps. A pool of light from her bedside lamp flooded onto the bed, making the patterned sheets jump out in vivid colors. Her mother held her hand and every so often stroked her face. "Dr. McGee should call back any minute now."

Kara felt tears trickle down her cheeks. "He's going to put me back in the hospital. Oh, Mom, I don't want to be sick. I hate CF." She didn't want to cry because crying only worsened her breathing problems, but she couldn't help herself. "I'm so tired of being sick. This was supposed to be such a great year."

Her mother dabbed Kara's face with a tissue. "I know, honey. But maybe they can clear up the infection quickly. You could still be back before Thanksgiving if you respond to the antibiotics."

"I wish Daddy were here."

"He's stuck in bad weather out in Chicago, but he'll get a flight back as soon as possible."

Kara wadded the bed linens with her fists. "It's not fair! Why am I being punished like this? What did I do to deserve this disease?"

She heard her mother's voice catch. "You didn't do anything, dear. If your dad and I weren't both carriers, if we only had known before we were married . . ." She allowed the sentence to trail.

"Are you sorry you had me?"

"Oh, no, baby. Never. Even seeing you suffer

could never make me wish you'd never been born. I love you so, Kara."

Kara twisted away. "Well, I wish I'd never been born."

"Please don't say that."

Kara turned her fevered face toward her mother. "I had such a good time tonight. It was like magic. I painted a bunch of little kids' faces. They were so cute. And then later, at the party, I danced with Eric, and we talked in the moonlight. Just for a little bit, I felt I was just an ordinary girl, flirting with a really cool guy. Oh, Mom, it was so perfect."

The phone on her bedside table rang. Her mother snatched up the receiver and after a short conversation hung up. "Dr. McGee wants us at the hospital right away. Can you manage in the car if I take you, or should I call the paramedics?" her mother asked.

Kara gritted her teeth and with pained effort forced herself upright. "No ambulance. I can make it. As long as I'm not unconscious, I'll go under my own steam."

Her mother helped her struggle to the door, stopping only long enough to grab a coat to cover Kara's thin frame.

Eleven

KARA FELT AS if she were suffocating, as if she were trying to breathe through a drinking straw. Her lungs felt on fire, and each breath was excruciating. Dr. McGee told her and her anxious parents, "It's viral pneumonia, bronchitis, and a staph infection. As you know, antibiotics won't touch the virus, but they'll help the others. We'll be doing cultures and blood gases, and, Kara, I'm putting you on a strong pain medication to help you relax and sleep."

"How long?" Kara managed to ask through her agony.

Dr. McGee arched an eyebrow. "I can't say how long it will take to get you on your feet again, but don't count on jumping out of here too soon. You're much sicker than when you were admitted last August." He patted her arm in a fond, fatherly gesture. "Have faith. We'll lick this infection."

Kara realized that she'd let the infection get out of control by refusing to call Dr. McGee when she first felt the sensations in her chest. She'd stubbornly hoped that it would go away with doses of cough syrup and daily respiratory therapy. She should have known better. "Sorry, Mom and Dad," she mumbled. "It's my fault I didn't catch the infection sooner."

"Don't blame yourself, honey," her father told her. He'd managed to grab a predawn flight and had arrived a few hours after Kara had been admitted. "You just get well."

"I'll spend a few nights here in the hospital with you," her mother told her. "You know they'll let me."

"But your job—"

"Can wait. You're my number-one priority."

Kara was torn between thinking she was too old to have her mother stay and wanting her to remain through the long nights, as she had when Kara had been a little girl. The child in Kara won out. "Just until I'm better."

"Not a minute more."

Kara squeezed her eyes shut as the painkiller stole over her body and pulled her toward a drugged sleep. "Can you get my schoolwork?"

"I'll call your teachers for your assignments."

"And my sketch pad—it's in my desk at home."

"I'll bring it later with your other things."

"We love you, honey. Just concentrate on getting well," Kara heard her mother say as sleep overcame her.

She drifted on a sea of fevered pain for five days, too sick to care much what was being done to her. They took blood with a long, sharp syringe from an artery in her groin. They pumped her full of medications and aerosol inhalants. Her veins kept collapsing, and they had to continually hunt for new ones to insert her IVs. Because she was so thin, every needle prick felt like a dagger being driven into her. She sucked on oxygen round the clock.

No visitors except her parents were admitted, for which she was grateful. She didn't want anyone—especially her friends—to see her suffering. Not Vince, who might have to go through it himself, and certainly not Eric or Elyse. Christy visited twice a day, held her hand, smoothed her sheets, and whispered words of encouragement. Kara couldn't speak—it took too much energy, too much air from lungs whose linings were raw and bleeding—but she offered mute thanks with her eyes.

Kara lost track of time, but did know that the nights seemed to stretch into eternity. She insisted that a light be kept on in her room, and since she slept fitfully, she'd startle awake, disoriented, and turn toward the circle of light like a ship seeking a safe harbor. Her mother slept on a roll-away bed, supplied by the hospital. In the long, lonely hours of darkness, when she couldn't sleep in spite of the drugs for pain, Kara listened to the slow rhythm of her mom's breathing, and found comfort in it.

If only she could breathe as easily! People took so many things about living for granted—like the simple act of breathing. It was an involuntary action. Even newborns did it without thinking about it. But for Kara, it was a battle. How she longed to breathe normally. Was it too much to ask for?

Dr. McGee came daily, wearing a perpetual frown between his gray eyes. He flipped through charts and file folders. She heard him tell nurses to switch medications, twice. She almost felt sorry for him because her particular collection of germs was frustrating his medical expertise. She wanted to apologize, but didn't have the energy to form the words.

She found herself silently repeating the Twenty-third Psalm. She wondered what heaven would be like and vowed to read her Bible more often when she recovered. She clung tenaciously to that goal—she *would* recover. "I've got so much left to do, God," she prayed silently in the long hours of the night when the fever gave her respite. "I'm only sixteen . . . but then, you know that. I'm not trying to be greedy, or tell you how to run the universe. But there's so much I want to do. I have a drawing to complete for a contest. I have my junior year to finish. I want to grow up and get fat.

"And my parents, they don't need this, either. Maybe they drive me crazy sometimes, and maybe I don't act it all the time, but I love them so much. Let me get well so they won't be sad.

"I almost had something going with this fabulous guy—maybe you know him—Eric Lawrence. Please, let me have another chance with him. He makes me feel so wonderful—like I'm floating and walking on clouds. I want to feel that way again. Just once more.

"Oh, and God, one more thing. I've got this friend, Vince. I know you know him because we've talked about you before. Please take special care of Vince. Don't let this happen to him. And let him find somebody who will care about him, be his friend, just in case I don't get better. But please, God, *please* let me be all right. Let me have tomorrow. Give me some time to have fun. I won't ask for anything else."

Kara was never certain when she turned the corner and began to rally. She only knew that the suffocating sensation slowly began to subside. Dr. McGee smiled when he visited her, still shuffling papers on her medical chart, which was the size of the phone book.

"You're definitely improving," Dr. McGee told her one morning. "Now, all you have to do is get your strength back."

Her mother looked a bit haggard, but she was all smiles. "Dad's been deadheading every flight so that he could come home as often as possible."

"How long has it been?" Kara asked. Her voice sounded hoarse and scratchy, like an old phonograph record.

Her mother patted her hand. "Two weeks. You've been here two weeks."

Kara felt dismayed. She'd come in on October 31, and now November was half gone. CF had robbed her yet again. Not only of strength and health and breath, but of time. And time was the one thing she was loath to relinquish. Tears started to slide down her cheeks. "I want to go home."

"Not yet," Dr. McGee said, touching her shoulder. "Hang on. I want you completely over this and back in your regular therapy regime before I release you. Be patient."

Kara's patience had run out. She ached from lying in bed. She was weak and shaky, and she knew without looking in a mirror that she'd dropped a lot more weight. Her overwhelming sense of frustration made her cry harder.

"You couldn't have visitors, dear, but you've got a ton of mail." Her mother's tone was cheery. "Do you feel up to sorting through some of it?"

The suggestion lifted Kara's spirits. "Yes," she whispered. "Help me sit up, please."

Her mother wedged pillows behind her back and shoulders as Dr. McGee slid his arms beneath her and boosted her upright. When she was comfortable, Dr. McGee said good-bye, and her mother brought in a sack of mail. Kara sorted through the collection, recognizing the handwriting of her grandparents, aunts and uncles, and family friends. Elyse had sent two cards. Her fingers fumbled awkwardly as she opened the envelope.

Kara,

I miss you! Please get well and come back to school. It's just the pits around here without you. I couldn't believe it when I couldn't even get in to visit you. I have to call your mom for reports. Vince is a basket case. He's been hanging around the hospital lobby, just in case you're able to see him. I'm trying to cheer him up.

Classes are a drag. I have a paper due in chemistry before Thanksgiving. My folks decided to visit my grandma in Virginia over the whole Christmas break. It won't be the same as staying here. Such a drag! Please call me the minute you can pick up a phone. Get well!

P.S. I'd mention Eric, but I know you don't want to hear about him.

Kara smiled, mentally hearing Elyse's chattering voice as she read. She counted fifteen cards from Vince—one for every day she'd been hospitalized, she guessed. She held one displaying a fuzzy teddy bear to her cheek and envisioned Vince buying it, writing it, mailing it. She felt lucky to have someone like Vince in her life.

Each card and letter touched her deeply. Yet, sick and weak as she was, she realized that there was nothing from the one person she'd hoped to hear from. Nothing to make her spirits sing and her heart happy. Not one thing from Eric Lawrence.

Twelve

CHRISTY CAME INTO the room and beamed Kara a smile. "Do you know how good it is to see you sitting up?" Kara returned Christy's hug and started clearing the mail off her bed. "Looks like the post office did a booming business on your behalf."

"I like getting cards," Kara confessed. "It makes me feel special."

"You are special." *Not special enough for Eric,* Kara thought. Christy's expression grew somber. "We were really concerned about you, Kara."

"We? You mean you and the doctors?"

"My brother, too."

Kara wanted to believe her, but figured she was only being polite. "Well, tell Eric the crisis is over."

"Your tone tells me that you don't believe me."

Kara shrugged. "You said all along that he wasn't the guy for me. You were right."

Christy plucked aimlessly at the bed sheet, the expression on her face pensive. "He took your hospitalization pretty hard. I could tell it was affecting him by the way he was acting. He either moped around or turned into a whirlwind of pointless activity. I made sure to give him a daily update on your condition."

Kara was careful to note that Christy never once said Eric had asked about her, only that she'd kept him informed.

"I think I owe you an apology," Christy continued slowly. "I should have stayed out of your relationship with Eric. You're a bright, mature girl and perfectly capable of making your own choices."

"That's nice of you to say, but it takes two to make a couple."

"I think I sold Eric short, too." Christy was struggling to put her thoughts into words, but Kara didn't know how to help her, so she kept silent and listened with all her heart. "He's having a tough time finding his place in the world. It's hard for him to express his feelings, but I know how deeply he feels things. I think it's a defense mechanism—if he doesn't *say* what he feels, then he doesn't have to deal with his feelings. It's much simpler for him to ease through life by pretending nothing matters. Even when something really does. Am I making any sense?"

Kara did understand, but found little comfort in the knowledge. Relationships took time, and time was something she was short on. "What you mean is that rather than taking the time to sort through feelings and hash out emotions, Eric avoids them altogether."

Christy flushed, and Kara knew her assessment was correct. "I'm not being disloyal to Eric. He and I have had some discussions about his—" she searched for a word, "—his cool attitude. My problem is, I love you both. I didn't want to see either of you get hurt."

"Too late," Kara told her.

Christy sighed and took Kara's hand. "Will you forgive me?"

Kara saw tears in Christy's eyes and realized she could never hold anything against her. Christy was the closest thing to a sister she would ever have. "Sure," Kara said. "I'm not mad at you. Eric has to make his own decisions."

"I love you," Christy said.

"I love you, too," Kara repeated, her voice thick with emotion.

Christy looked relieved, and her face brightened. "Listen. How about if I check with Dr. McGee and see if it's okay for you to go outside tomorrow?"

"Could you?" Through her window, Kara saw the gray November sky and the tops of trees. One of the best things about the hospital was its beautiful wooded property and footpaths. Often, patients were allowed to go outside accompanied by a nurse or a health care worker.

"I'll get a wheelchair and take you on a grand tour. You'll have to bundle up."

"No problem. Mom's brought half my wardrobe."

They laughed, but then Christy's expression grew serious again. "It's so good to have you back with us. You're a real fighter, and I knew you wouldn't give up. I would give anything if I could do something for you, Kara—if I could take away your CF forever."

"I've got another chance," Kara said. "It's what I wanted. And as long as I get it, I'm going to take it."

That evening, Vince came to see Kara. "I've missed you," he said, and kissed her forehead. "Do you know how scared I was?"

Delighted by his show of affection, Kara gave him a radiant smile. "I fooled them," she said, pulling away and looking up into Vince's dark eyes. "They didn't think I could get on top of this one, but I did."

"You look wonderful."

She made a face. "Don't lie to me, even out of kindness. I know how I look." She settled back onto her pillows, still holding his hand. "Speaking of looking good . . . You look super."

He gave a self-conscious shuffle. "This is the best autumn I've ever had with my CF. No new infections and a hardy appetite. For once, the enzyme pills are doing their thing. I've gained some weight."

"It's more than that. You look—" she fished for a word,—"bigger."

"I've got a secret." He glanced about conspiratorially, even though they were alone in the room. "I've been lifting weights in the gym after school."

"I had no idea."

"Well, it's no big deal. I didn't know if my lungs could handle it, but the more I build myself up, the better I do. The doctor says it's fine for me to continue."

"Maybe I should try."

He laughed. "You couldn't even lift a dumbbell right now."

"Could, too." She gave him a sidelong glance. "I lifted *you* up, didn't I? In spirit, of course."

His dark eyes twinkled. "Yes, you did. I'm so high now, I feel like I'm flying."

"Thanks for all the cards," she said. "Fifteen! I'm touched."

He bowed stiffly from the waist. "You're more than worth it. Did you get any others—you know from kids at school?"

"Elyse."

"And?"

She knew what he was fishing for, and trying not to sound dejected, she said, "No, Eric didn't send me anything.

"I didn't mean him."

She stared at him keenly. "Yes, you did. It's not

important, okay? I would have been more shocked if he had sent me one."

"He's an idiot."

"No," she corrected. "He's not sick. You can't expect him to understand our world."

"Don't make excuses for him," Vince argued.

She held up her hand. "Stop. I don't want to talk about him." She smiled and squeezed Vince's hand. "Let's change the subject. I want to think of some dastardly prank to play on the nurses. Like the time we were hospitalized at the same time when we were kids and we smeared Vaseline on all the doorknobs." She slugged Vince playfully. "Help me come up with something."

Kara lay awake, staring up at the ceiling and listening to the night sounds of the hospital. There was the hum of the central heating unit and the muffled sound from a radio at the nurses' station. Occasionally, she heard a nurse pass down the hall and the soft squeak of rubber-soled shoes on the linoleum. The light burned dimly in the hall, and from somewhere down the corridor, Kara heard a child crying for its mother.

She sighed and shifted upright. No use trying to go back to sleep. She knew from experience, sleep wouldn't come anytime soon. She decided that if she had to be awake, she should keep herself busy and catch up on her schoolwork. She was behind in every subject. With a sigh, she opened the drawer of her bedside table, where she'd left her work.

Inside the drawer, she noticed a long, elegant envelope lying on top of her English book. She picked it up and read her name, which had been written across the front in calligraphed letters. The envelope was of fine parchment paper, and it had been sealed with red wax, stamped with the letters OLW.

Odd, she thought. She'd been positive she'd opened all her mail. How could this one have gotten past her? How had it gotten into the drawer? Kara gingerly broke the red seal and pulled out two pieces of paper. One was a letter written in delicate script. The other was a check made out in her name for an enormous sum of money. She stared openmouthed.

Quickly Kara picked up the letter, and using the soft glow of the light on the wall over her bed, she began to read.

Dear Kara,

You don't know me, but I know about you and because I do I want to give you a special gift. Accompanying this letter is a certified check, my gift to you with no strings attached to spend on anything you want. No one knows about this gift except you, and you are free to tell anyone you want.

Who I am isn't really important, only that you and I have much in common. Through no fault of our own we have endured pain and isolation and have spent many days in a hospital feeling lonely and scared. I hoped for a miracle, but most of all

I hoped for someone to truly understand what I was going through.

I can't make you live longer. I can't stop you from hurting, but I can give you one wish as someone did for me. My wish helped me find purpose, faith, and courage.

Friendship reaches beyond time and the true miracle is in giving, not receiving. Use my gift to fulfill your wish.

Your forever friend,
JWC

Flabbergasted, Kara reread the letter and stared at the check. It was made out in her name. She counted the zeros. One hundred thousand dollars. It seemed real, but incredible at the same time. Who could JWC possibly be? The check was signed, "Richard Holloway, Esq., Administrator, One Last Wish Foundation."

Kara was awestruck. She felt as if she were in a movie or TV show. She looked around the room, but no one shouted, "Surprise!" With trembling fingers, Kara slid the letter and check back inside the envelope. Her schoolwork forgotten, she stared thoughtfully into space. What she wanted more than anything else was to be well, but no amount of money could buy that. Still, there were plenty of things she could do. She wanted to share this incredible event with someone—but who? She decided that her parents would be skeptical of the entire mysterious business, even though the check looked real. Should she tell Christy? Elyse? Vince or Eric? Finally, she decided to take her time and think it through thoroughly. This was a miracle and she didn't want to do anything foolish.

Kara turned out the light, and cradling the letter to her chest, she fell asleep.

Thirteen

ERIC EASED THE heavy barbells back into their slots on the weight lifting bench and felt the exhilaration that came from pumping iron. He wiped the sweat from his face with a nearby towel. "Not bad," his spotter said. "That's the most repetitions you've done this week."

He draped the towel over his neck and stood. Across the gym, he saw Vince, struggling to do arm curls with a set of barbells. When Vince had first appeared at the extracurricular weight lifting program in the school gym, Eric and the others had been skeptical. Now, watching Vince fight for breath as he lifted, Eric felt a grudging admiration for him. Vince wasn't a quitter, and he was making progress. Eric could see how Vince's upper body was developing through the course of his workouts.

Eric thought better of going over to Vince. Except for having to see each other in English class, they steered clear of each other. Ever since the night of Howie's party, Eric had felt uncomfortable around Vince. Eric went inside the locker room; he had showered and dressed and was ready to leave when Vince came over to him. "You got a minute?" Vince asked.

"Sure. What do you need? Is it about an English assignment?"

"No. I want to talk to you."

"I'm listening."

The noisy locker room was beginning to fill up. Vince glanced around. "Not here. Want some pizza? I'll buy."

The thought of pizza made Eric hungry, and he was curious about what Vince wanted to discuss. "Sounds all right. My car's out in the lot."

"You'll have to drop me back here to pick up mine after we eat."

"No problem."

They walked out into the blustery day, and Eric raised the collar of his sheepskin jacket to ward off the chill. Once the two of them were in Eric's Chevy, Vince directed him toward a pizza parlor. Feeling somewhat uncomfortable, Eric flipped on the radio and turned it up loud.

At the nearly empty restaurant, they chose a booth and ordered. While they waited for their pizza, Eric fidgeted with a paper napkin. "So, what's up?" Eric finally asked.

"Kara."

Eric felt confusion, then a small stab of fear. "She's still doing okay, isn't she?"

"Do you care?"

"Now, wait a minute—"

Vince leaned forward, close to Eric's face. "*You* wait a minute. For reasons that make no sense to me, Kara likes you. I've got some things to say to you, and so hear me out."

Eric swallowed, unsure of how to respond. "I like Kara," he said, shredding the paper napkin into strips.

"With friends like you, who needs enemies?" Vince said sarcastically. A flare of anger shot through Eric, but before he could react, Vince added, "Do you know what that girl's been through these last few weeks?"

"Christy told me—"

"No matter what your sister's told you, you don't know the half of it. I've been there, so I *do* know, and now I'm going to tell you. When you're hospitalized with CF, you feel as if you're drowning in your own body fluids. For every day you're lying in that bed, the nights stretch twice as long. You're scared because there're no guarantees that your doctor's bag of tricks will work this time—it seems that the nasty little germs get more resistant every time they're faced with a new antibiotic." Vince ticked off points on his fingers as he spoke. Eric sat quietly, not interrupting.

"I know what it feels like to think that everybody in the world's having a good time but you because the only faces you see are nurses and doctors and lab techs who poke you full of needles and suck blood out of you until it hurts so bad, you think you're going to scream.

"I know what it's like to cough up your guts and vomit blood. And I know how it feels when you wake up one morning and realize you're still alive and that you made it through one more episode, only to know that you'll have to do it all over again. Until the one day you don't wake up at all."

Eric had broken out in a cold sweat, but he kept his expression stony, ashamed of the revulsion he was feeling as Vince's words bombarded him. Poor Kara. Poor Vince.

Vince leaned back against the booth, as if the explanation had drained him of energy. "When you're recovering, days turn into years. The only thing that keeps you from suicide is seeing friendly faces. Every time I've been through it during the last four years, Kara's been there for me. And I've been there for her. This time, I was, too."

"I-I'm glad—"

Vince pinned him with a look. "But she doesn't want me. She wants you." Finally, he looked out the window, his face dark with misery.

"I thought she was your girl," Eric mumbled.

"No, you didn't. You were just too much of a coward to go after her."

If any other guy had called him a coward, Eric

would have decked him. But Vince had bared his soul, and Eric knew everything he'd said was true. He *was* a coward, unwilling to become involved on more than a superficial level because he was afraid of sickness, of suffering. Kara had reached out to him the first day of school. He had responded, but when he learned about her problems, he had retreated.

"What should I do?" Eric asked.

"Figure something out on your own, Eric. Don't expect me to make it easy for you. This is one of the hardest things I've ever done, but I'm doing it for Kara."

The pizza came, and they ate in silence. Eric barely tasted it. He wanted to tell Vince that he was sorry and that he did care about Kara. She was sweet and decent and kind, and he had blown it.

He remembered the night of Howie's party. She'd felt feather light and fragile in his arms when they danced. In the moonlight, she'd looked wispy soft and beautiful. That night, the monster disease that lived inside her had been eating her lungs alive. She had been fighting for every breath, and he'd never realized it.

He should have been reaching out to her all this time instead of avoiding her, pretending she didn't matter. He was ashamed that he'd acted as if her sickness was her fault. He stared at Vince, wanting to find words to explain it to him, but he couldn't. "I do care," he said, but the words sounded hollow and flat.

"Caring is *doing,* Eric. It's not some head game. It's doing something that says, 'I care.' Lots of people are turned off by CF—by sick people in general. It's okay if you can't handle it, but don't lead someone on. Don't play games."

Eric had no comeback for Vince, no defense and no excuses. He hadn't meant to hurt Kara. It was just so hard for him to give free rein to his feelings.

After they finished, they walked to Eric's car, and he drove Vince back to his car. Eric switched on the heater, hoping to warm up the car, but realized that the cold feeling was coming from within.

At the school parking lot, as Vince opened the door to slide out, his knee accidentally hit the button on Eric's glove compartment. It flopped open, and when the contents spilled on the floor, Vince reached to pick things up. A bright blue envelope was addressed to Kara.

"A get well card," Eric mumbled by way of explanation. He had intended to do something for Kara. Surely, Vince could see that.

"Did you forget your way to the mailbox?" Vince got out of the car and tossed the card onto the seat. "No guts, Eric, my man. That's your problem. No guts."

Eric watched Vince walk to his car, climb in, and drive away. Eric sat staring out into the darkness until the chill began to permeate his thick jacket. He felt cold, and alone.

Fourteen

KARA SPENT THE morning thinking about what she should do with her wish money. She still hadn't told anyone and felt frustrated. She decided to give her mind a rest and occupy herself with drawing. Now she sat in the hospital sun room in a wheelchair, her sketch pad spread across her lap. Deep in concentration, she moved her pencil quickly, coaxing the image in her mind to appear on the white surface. Her brow furrowed. She didn't even look up when she heard someone enter the room. She was ready for the ride around the grounds that Christy had promised her at lunchtime. Maybe she'd confide in Christy concerning the letter she told herself.

"You look serious," Eric said.

For a moment, she thought she might have

imagined him. She started, almost dropping the pad.

"Have I changed that much in three weeks?" he asked.

Her heart beat crazily, and a smile lit up her face. "I didn't expect you. It's great to see you. Of course, you haven't changed. Why are you here?"

"To check on you." His hands were shoved in the pockets of his jacket. He came over to her, and she closed the pad swiftly. He was as handsome as she remembered . . . more so. "I'm sorry I didn't come sooner."

Something in the hesitancy of his tone of voice made her realize that he thought she might send him away. The notion surprised her. She could never do such a thing. Seeing Eric made her feel as if a surge of electricity had shot through her. "You're here now. That's what matters."

He knelt beside the chair and touched the back of her hand, black and blue from IV needles. "You should see my ankles," she said with a self-conscious laugh.

"No, thanks." He looked her full in the face, and she felt as if her heart had taken up residency in her throat. "I'm glad you're feeling better."

"Me, too."

"Want to go for a ride?"

"With you?"

"Christy told me she was scheduled to take you outside. I'd like to take you instead—if you're up to it."

Up to it, Kara thought. She'd been dreaming of it. "I really would like to go out."

He stood. "Do you have a coat? Even though the sun's shining, it's pretty cold."

She was wearing a thick cable-stitched blue sweater, but she knew he was right. "There's a jacket in my room."

He pushed her down the hall, passing several nurses who waved. In her room, he helped her into a bulky ski jacket and laid a blanket over her knees, carefully tucking it around her legs. Then he pushed her toward the elevators. She would have given anything to be walking alongside of him, but it was out of the question.

In the lobby, people hurried past. She watched them, envious of their ability to move and breathe at the same time. "There are trails all along the grounds," she told Eric. "Sometimes, you even forget you're near a hospital."

Outside, the air was sharp and cold, and it stung her lungs. She swallowed the urge to cough. Pale sunlight flickered through bare tree branches as she looked skyward. When she'd been hospitalized, it had been autumn and the leaves had been brilliant shades of red and gold and orange. Now, they all lay on the ground in heaps, dry and papery, blown about by northern winds.

"You're quiet," Eric said. "Anything wrong?"

"I was just thinking that I've gone and missed autumn this year. I hate that. Did you know that if a person lives a hundred years, he only gets to see the leaves change colors a hundred times? That doesn't seem like much, does it?"

"Not when you put it that way. I guess I take it for granted. Autumn comes. Autumn goes."

"I never take autumn for granted," she said. "It's beautiful and my very favorite time of year."

"I like summer. No school."

"Summer's nice. Houston's near the Gulf, isn't it?"

"It's not too far a drive. My friends and I used to hang out plenty at the beach."

"Do you miss Houston?"

"A little."

"Will you be going back when school's out?" she asked, but he didn't reply right away. At least, he was with her now. If he was going back, she didn't want to know.

"Summer seems a long way off in November. Too far to make plans now."

Vince had once told her the same thing. *No use making plans with anyone,* she told herself. "There's a rest area. Why don't we park for a minute. You can sit on one of the benches, and we can talk."

"But we've hardly made a dent in the path."

She wanted to look at him, be with him, not just hear his voice over her head. "I'd like to stop rolling for a minute," she said lightly. "A person could get motion sickness doing any kind of speed in one of these things."

He parked the chair and set the brake, then brushed dead leaves off one of the benches and sat down in front of her. "Are you sure you're not cold?"

"Not a bit," she lied. Truth was, it now hurt to breathe.

He picked a fallen leaf from her blond hair. "A souvenir from an autumn gone bye-bye," he said, handing it to her.

"I'll put it in my scrapbook when I get home."

"Any idea when that will be?"

"Dr. McGee is acting like a sphinx. I ask, but can't pin him down."

Eric glanced at his watch and jerked upright. "Oh, my gosh, I promised Christy I'd have you back in twenty minutes. We've been gone over thirty."

She wasn't sure if he was telling her that because it was true, or if he was bored. "I'll tell her it was my fault. Don't worry."

Eric took off the brake and started the chair back toward the hospital. "You don't know my sister. She'll have my butt."

Kara giggled. "I can't believe you're scared of Christy."

"Are you kidding? She's a terror. She cracks her whip, and I have to jump. I do laundry, cleaning, and cooking like a slave."

"Should I report her to the authorities for child abuse?"

"Don't laugh. I'm telling you, she's tough."

By the time they got back to Kara's room, Eric's outrageous tales of his life with Christy had Kara laughing so hard, she couldn't catch her breath.

Eric rolled her inside and came to a screeching stop. Vince was waiting.

"Looks like I missed a good joke," he said, his eyes on Kara.

She reached out to him, and he bent down and hugged her. "Eric's been telling me how Christy's turned him into a slave."

"He looks abused," Vince said drolly, unzipping Kara's jacket and helping her take it off. "Glad you could make it," Vince added to Eric.

Kara sensed an undercurrent between them. "You two haven't been arguing at school, have you?"

"No," they said in unison.

"Help me get back in bed," she said, suddenly struggling for breath. "I guess I'm not used to so much fresh air." She wanted to cough hard and would have if it had been only Vince in the room with her.

Eric scooped her up in his arms, and Vince pulled aside the covers. Eric placed her down gently, and Vince draped the covers around her body. "Such teamwork," she said.

"Well, if it isn't Dopey and Grumpy," Christy said to Eric and Vince as she breezed into the room. She came swiftly to Kara's bedside. "I was checking to make sure you were all right."

"I'm in good hands."

"Dr. McGee wants some more chest X rays right away. I told the tech I'd bring you down."

Kara groaned her displeasure. She was so tired.

Even the little bit of exercise she'd done had wiped her out. "Do I have to?"

"Yes, you have to," Vince said. "Eric will put you back in the chair."

"We can wait here until you come up again," Eric offered.

"No," Kara said wearily. "Do me a favor. Go take each other out for a soda. Pretend I'm with you. Then come by tomorrow and tell me how much I enjoyed myself. I feel better just knowing you're together having fun."

Eric and Vince exchanged glances. "That what you want?" Vince asked.

Kara nodded. "Maybe Dr. McGee will give me a pass this Saturday." She turned to Christy. "Will you help me persuade him? Just for a few hours?"

"A pass?" Eric asked.

"Sometimes the doctor will let us check out of the hospital to take in a movie or something. We're not well enough to go home, but we're not sick enough to be penned up on this floor twenty-four hours a day, either. It keeps us from going stir-crazy," Vince explained.

"And the nurses from throwing us out a window," Kara joked. "Sometimes we can act pretty rank."

"Let's see how you're doing after your morning treatment," Christy urged. She shooed the boys toward the door once Eric had settled Kara back into her wheelchair for the ride down to X Ray.

"Don't forget," Kara said. "Go have a soda for me."

Once they were gone, Christy pushed her down the corridor to the elevator and down to the lab, without conversation. Kara felt bone-weary and a little apprehensive about the timing on the X rays. She wondered why Dr. McGee ordered that they be done immediately. She hadn't had a chance to tell anyone about the letter and check. She wondered if the mysterious JWC had felt as physically drained as she was feeling. JWC were the initials. JWC had been in hospitals and endured pain. *JWC, whoever you are,* Kara thought, *please know how much I appreciate you, your letter, and your gift.*

Fifteen

WHEN DR. MCGEE allowed Kara a four-hour pass for Saturday afternoon, she was ecstatic. She made plans with Eric and Vince. They picked her up in Eric's car and drove to the mall with the eight-choice movie theater. "Too bad this isn't a convertible," she said as she sat between them in the front seat, feeling as if she'd been sprung from jail.

"Are you kidding?" Eric said. "We'd freeze to death in a convertible."

"But it's a beautiful day," she cried, hugging her arms to herself. "A beautiful day to be alive. Life is full of surprises, you know."

Eric glanced toward Vince. "I think she's gone bonkers, Vince. What about you?"

"Totally stark raving mad," Vince said with an

easy smile. "In case you haven't noticed, Miss Fischer, it's raining."

She ducked her head to peer at the sky through the windshield. Raindrops beat a steady patter on the glass. "Liquid sunshine. It's all in your perspective, you know."

"Well, Vince, why don't you grab the umbrella in the backseat to ward off the liquid rays while I park the car." Eric had pulled up at the mall entrance nearest the movie theaters. Vince found the umbrella, helped Kara out of the car, and walked her to the entrance. "See you in a sec!" Eric yelled to them.

Inside, the mall was swarming with people. The merchants had already put up Christmas decorations, although Thanksgiving was still a week away. A giant Christmas tree glittered with lights, and music played from the sound system. As they approached the theater entrance, Kara savored the smell of buttered popcorn.

"Are you all right?" Vince asked.

"I thought you weren't going to ask me that every five minutes," she countered.

"I'm not."

"Then stop it right now."

"Sorry."

She felt bad about snapping at him, but he was beginning to sound like her parents. "Are *you* all right?"

Vince took her hand. "I've never been better. The monster sleeps."

Lucky, she thought. Eric jogged up beside them.

"Let's get our tickets. Do you want to see a comedy, horror, or what?"

Kara hesitated. "Listen, I don't really feel like sitting through a movie—any movie at all."

"Are you sick?" Vince asked, looking anxious.

"I can get the car," Eric added.

In exasperation, Kara put her hands on her hips and glared at Vince and Eric. "Now, listen, I'm not a breakable doll. I've been sick, but Dr. McGee wouldn't have let me out if he didn't think I could handle it. I don't need the two of you fussing over me."

"I think we're in trouble," Eric said to Vince.

"She looks so small and defenseless, too," Vince replied.

"Like a pit bull," Eric said.

Kara flashed a sheepish grin. "Okay. I know you mean well. But this is my first day of freedom in a month. I've changed my mind, and I really don't want to be sitting in a dark theater."

"So what do you want to do?" Vince asked.

"I'd like to go to the food court and get ice cream with gobs of fudge sauce."

"She's hungry?" Eric asked Vince.

"Don't knock it," Vince insisted.

Kara wasn't really hungry, but she wanted to be with Vince and Eric and share time talking with them. She wasn't sure if she'd tell them about her anonymous letter, but she needed to talk. They went to the center of the mall and found a table. Kara waited while Vince and Eric bought ice cream concoctions and brought them to her. She scooped up a mouthful of the fudge sauce and smiled at both boys, who were watching her. "It's delicious," she said. Maybe her appetite would return faster than it had in the past following hospitalizations.

Christmas music played in the background, and twinkle lights hung on trees and bushes in the planters. "The Christmas season starts earlier every year," Vince said between bites of his banana split. "But I never do my shopping until Christmas Eve, anyway."

"I usually wait until the day after," Eric kidded. "It's cheaper."

Kara shook her head at them. "What Scrooges you both are. Christmas is fabulous. I love Christmas trees and presents and all the trimmings. What's Santa going to bring you guys this year?"

"I don't want much of anything," Vince said. "Maybe some compact discs and a new sweater or two."

"Speak for yourself," Eric interrupted. "I want Santa to help me get my car painted. A paint job—a good one—costs a mint."

"Boy, you two think small," Kara chided. "I want a trip around the world, expensive jewelry, a new wardrobe, and a night out dancing I'll never forget."

Eric tipped back in his chair. "As long as we're talking fantasyland, then I want my own car dealership so I can sell Ferraris, Lamborghinis, and restored classics."

"Boring," Vince said with a wave of his hand. "That's hard work. I'd like to star in the next Arnold Schwarzenegger film." When Eric and Kara laughed, he added, "Okay, I'll settle for directing his next film." Vince paused. "What the heck, I'd like to *be* Arnold."

By now, Kara and Eric were laughing hard. "Not even Santa can bring that to pass."

Vince stood. "You don't think Santa can do this? Come on. He's right over there. Let's go ask him." Vince pointed across the mall to the area where long lines of children were waiting to meet Santa.

"Good idea," Kara said, starting toward the end of the line.

Eric and Vince dogged after her. They stood in line, despite the stares of small children, and when they reached Santa, who was perched on a painted gold throne, they had their pictures taken with him.

Vince glanced at his watch. "Only an hour left of freedom, Kara. Where to now?"

Kara didn't want to think about returning to the hospital, even though she was tired and short of breath. She wished the afternoon could go on forever. She wanted to tell everyone who passed them, "I'm so happy! Isn't life wonderful?" She'd decided against telling Vince and Eric about the letter she'd received, but she had an idea now that pleased her.

On the way back to the car, they passed a video

arcade and decided to stop. They played three-way games of Laser Tag, and when Kara grew tired, she sat and watched Vince and Eric pile up points, vying for top score.

They'd just finished playing every game in the arcade, when Eric noticed a machine that required a player to try to lift a toy with a robot hand and drop it into a slot for retrieval. "Think I can do it in three tries?" he asked.

"I never could," Vince admitted. "I'm telling you, it eats quarters like candy."

Eric eyed the large glass case, jammed with toys. "How hard can it be? Which one do you want, Kara?"

She studied the jumble of stuffed toys and pointed to a red satin heart-shaped pillow trimmed in white lace. "That looks pretty tacky, but I love it. Can you get it for me?"

Vince lent Eric a quarter, and when the machine hummed to life, Eric artfully maneuvered the robot hand directly over the pillow, lowered it carefully, and made a grab for it. He missed. Kara groaned. "Have faith," Eric muttered, his brow furrowed in concentration.

"No way he can do it on a single quarter," said a boy who had come over to watch.

Kara crossed her fingers, and Eric lowered the arm and squeezed the robot tongs via the remote control again.

"Two strikes," another boy said when he missed the second time.

"Last try," Vince warned. "Come on, man, you can do it."

Eric carefully repositioned the arm, lowered it one final time, and snagged the edge of the lace. The kids gasped as he ever so slowly inched it over to the retrieval slot. The pillow dangled, hung by a thread, then fell neatly into the hole. The audience cheered as Eric scooped it out, raised his arms like a victorious prizefighter, then presented it to Kara with a flourish.

She laughed and cuddled the satin prize to her cheek. "It's perfect," she told him.

He grabbed her, lifted her off the floor, and whirled her around. From the corner of her eyes, she caught Vince's face, his smile looking tight. When Eric put her down, she went over and put her arms around him. "Your quarter made it possible."

Ten minutes later, they started back to the hospital. The rain had stopped, and puddles reflected sunlight from the late afternoon sky as they crossed from the parking lot to the hospital entrance. Back in her room, Kara turned to Eric and Vince. "It was a perfect day. Thank you."

Once they left, a sense of melancholy stole over her. More than anything, she longed to go with them. She wanted out of the hospital. She wanted to spend Thanksgiving at home. She wanted so many things. An hour before, she'd been on top of the world, and now she felt in the depths of depression.

She thought about the One Last Wish money,

hidden in her drawer. "Soon," she promised herself. She'd tell her parents, because now she had a plan. She held the small satin heart against her face while tears of loneliness slid slowly down her cheeks.

Sixteen

KARA AWOKE TO the aroma of roasting turkey. She stretched, luxuriating in the feel of her own bed, the surroundings of her own room. She was glad to be home, even if she couldn't stay long. Dr. McGee had released her for the holiday, but had asked that she return on Monday.

"But why?" She'd felt dismayed. "I thought I was better."

"We've licked this infection, but we've discovered another problem. I've already been over it with your parents. I told them I would explain it to you."

Kara swallowed hard. Her father had come to sign her out and take her home. "Tell me," Kara told Dr. McGee.

"The last round of X rays showed that the right

side of your heart is enlarged. It's a condition called cor pulmonale. Lung damage from the CF means less oxygen is getting into your blood. That's making your heart work harder and increasing your blood pressure."

"My heart—that sounds serious."

"It is," Dr. McGee admitted frankly. "I've asked a cardiologist to consult on your case."

Kara looked around her bedroom and shoved the conversation out of her mind. She concentrated on the aromas of turkey and pumpkin pie. A tightness constricted her chest, and she wondered if she'd ever wake up and not feel she needed air the way a person dying of thirst craves water.

Elyse and her family were away for the weekend, but Vince checked in with an early call. "I want to come see you, but Mom's being a pain," he told Kara. "She won't let any of us go anywhere. I think it's some crazy thing she has about us all being together on holidays. She acts as if each holiday's our last one."

"No problem," Kara told him, understanding perfectly his mother's fears. Her mother treated holidays in the same way. Family time was everything. "Come over sometime this weekend."

Kara had thought about inviting Christy and Eric to join them, but before she could, Christy had confided, "I promised I'd work for a fellow therapist who wants to take a long weekend. I don't have to check in till four, so I'm fixing turkey with all the trimmings. You know, Eric and I haven't had Thanksgiving together in three years, and I hope we'll be able to talk. Besides, if I cook, I'll have leftovers. Believe me, my kid brother can eat!" Christy had added with a laugh.

Kara and her parents ate their Thanksgiving meal early in the day. Her mother had fixed enough food to feed half the city's homeless. Kara felt sorry that she could only nibble, but she'd been on liquid supplements and intravenous fluids so long that even small quantities of solid food—as tasty as her mother's cooking was—filled her up. She spent the rest of the day curled up on the sofa watching football games on TV with her dad while her mother sat beside her, sewing a needlepoint cushion.

That night, as her mother finished administering her thumps, Kara climbed into bed and kissed her mother on the cheek. "This was a perfect Thanksgiving. I hope we have more just like it."

"You sound rather sentimental," her mother said as she sat down on the bed. "Not that I mind," she added hastily, "but it's not like you."

"I'm glad to be home. I'm glad you and Dad are my parents. I was thinking that maybe I didn't tell you often enough how much you mean to me." She wanted to confide in her mother about the One Last Wish letter, but the timing didn't seem right. Besides, Kara felt tired, not up to a long discussion about it.

Her mother stroked Kara's hair. "I'm glad you're our daughter."

"Are you sorry you didn't have more children?"

"Yes, sometimes, but Dad and I made the right choice for us."

Kara realized why she had been an only child. CF was passed to children by two parents who were both carriers of a special recessive gene. While neither parent had the disease, they could pass it on to their children. Her parents always faced the risk of having other CF children, and she understood why they never took the chance.

Kara gazed thoughtfully at her mother. "I would love to have a baby one day. Wouldn't you like grandkids, Mom?"

"No time soon," her mother said with a laugh. "You have plenty of time to get married and have kids. Don't rush it."

Kara wanted to believe her. She looked into her mother's eyes and saw sadness. Both of them knew the medical odds facing Kara's future. "Don't worry. I haven't even got a steady boyfriend," Kara said quickly, not wanting to see her mother depressed. "Maybe I never will." Kara considered bringing up the incredible news of the letter she received, but found herself holding back.

"Vince likes you."

"I like Vince, but not in that way."

"You'll find someone special," her mother assured her. "It takes time."

Time, Kara thought. Everything always comes back to having more time.

When the doorbell rang Friday morning Kara was surprised, then thrilled. Eric dropped by unexpectedly. He met her parents, and after a few minutes of fidgeting while they chatted, he took a deep breath and asked, "Could Kara and I do something together? Christy took more overtime at the hospital. I don't want to spend the day alone."

More than anything, Kara wanted to be with Eric. "I'd love to go," she said quickly. Her mother was hesitant, but her father flashed a "leave her be" look. Kara left with a promise to be home at a reasonable hour. One of them would have to get up to administer her thumps, but Eric didn't need to know about that.

Eric headed out of the city down winding country highways, the radio playing and the car heater keeping them toasty warm. Kara watched the rolling Tennessee countryside slip past, and even though the hills were brown and dry, she thought they looked beautiful. Eric pulled over, and they found a footpath and slowly walked through the woods. In spite of her heavy jacket, she shivered. Eric put his arm around her and pulled her close. His big, warm body protected her from the chill, and she hated to go back to the car.

"Will you come back to Christy's with me?" he asked. "We can light a fire in the fireplace and spread blankets on the floor. We'll have a picnic."

"Sounds perfect to me."

If he'd offered her a flight to the moon, she'd have gone. It didn't matter where they were together, just as long as she could be with him.

At Christy's apartment, he carted logs to the

fireplace and lit them. She heard the wind whistle by the windows and shivered. She stretched out on the floor, propping herself up with pillows to make breathing easier. "Sure you don't want some?" Eric asked, offering her a bite of the sandwich he'd created for himself. It was tall as a tower. "Turkey's much better the next day, you know."

"I know," she said, "but no, thanks."

"You haven't eaten all day."

"I don't eat much."

"We've got some marshmallows to roast later."

"I'll have some of those." She figured she could manage a few gooey marshmallows. She stared into the fire and watched the pale yellow flames dance. "I have to go back to the hospital on Monday," she said.

"Christy told me." He stretched out on his side next to her, his head resting on one propped up arm. "I think it's lousy. Don't you ever get angry about having CF?"

"Sure I do. But it doesn't change it. Besides, it's a part of me." She turned her face toward his and touched the hair on his forehead, flecked with firelight. "It's like being born with brown hair. Or blue eyes. Having CF isn't something a person has a choice about."

"I know it's not your fault you're sick," he insisted.

"It's just something that *happens* to a person. I mean, I could have been born to other parents. But then I wouldn't be me, would I?"

"But it's not fair."

She smiled knowingly, remembering all the times she'd used that same phrase in frustration. "You're right, it isn't fair. I didn't even *know* I was sick until I was at least six years old."

"How could you not know?"

She turned her gaze on the fire. "For as long as I can remember, I've had someone pounding on my back and chest two to three times a day. I've had to cough in order to breathe and take pills before meals. For a long time, I didn't question it. I didn't know that every other little kid in the world didn't do the same things every day. I thought all kids were exactly like me."

"But they aren't." He toyed with a lock of her hair.

"I began to notice," she said. "*I* was the one who was different. And I hated it. Even though I was small at the time, and I didn't understand it fully, I got real angry about it. I would hide when it came time for my therapy. I'd kick and scream at my parents and call them mean names. Sometimes I made my mother cry."

Eric smoothed the lock of hair behind her ear. "Funny, you don't look like a meany to me."

She shook her head and looked up into his face. "I was awful. I hated everybody, and yet I was dependent on them, too. Without the thumps, I couldn't breathe. A person gets addicted to breathing, you know."

"Thump or die, huh?" He chuckled.

"Exactly. Except that some days the thumps aren't enough. I was in and out of the hospital six times when I was twelve. No matter what I did, my lungs kept betraying me. About that same time, I decided I must be a most terrible person and that I was being punished. I believed that God hated me."

"I'd probably think the same thing."

"I met Vince during that phase. He had CF like me, and so we used to talk about God and having CF and feeling cursed." She looked at Eric, her expression shy. "We made some earth-shattering discoveries about life."

"I'd like to hear them," Eric said.

"We decided that everybody suffers one way or another at some point in their lives. Nobody gets away scot-free. Suffering is just something people have to do—a kind of dues paying for the privilege of living and being happy. And sometimes it seems to me until you know the one—suffering—you can't know the other—happiness. It's like they play off each other. Do you know what I mean?"

"I understand, but I don't know why you have to suffer so much and someone else—someone who's a jerk or a creep—like a murderer—doesn't seem to suffer much at all."

"There you go again," Kara chided, while toying with the edge of the blanket. "You're asking that life be 'fair.' Nobody knows how much anybody else hurts. We can't walk around in another person's skin—not even for a moment. Sometimes, people reach out, and that's really special. But we just have to look for happiness in each day, no matter what's happening to us."

"Are you happy now?"

She watched the firelight reflect in his eyes. Inside, she felt a melting sensation, as if she might dissolve and soak into the floor. She raised one trembling finger and traced the outline of his mouth. "Yes. I'm happy now."

He caught her hand and held it. "Kara, I've never known anybody like you."

"You mean a terribly skinny girl with scratchy breathing?"

He lowered his ear to her chest, resting his head ever so gently. "It sounds to me like a kitten purring."

Kara touched his hair, and he raised his head and stared into her eyes. Eric lowered his mouth to hers, hesitantly at first, barely brushing her lips. He cradled her head on his arm and stroked her hair with his free hand. She felt warm and protected, totally lost in his embrace. He drew back and stared down at her, his gaze serious. "Kara, I don't want to—"

She silenced him by kissing him fully. Not once in all her life had she experienced the sensations pouring through her now in Eric's arms, and she didn't want them to end. "Hold me," she whispered. "Please hold me."

His arms slipped around her. She clung to him

fiercely while her breath came raggedly. She was so filled with wanting and yearning that she ached. She heard the crackling fire, the howling wind. Time seemed to stand still. She raised her head and offered her lips for Eric's lingering kiss.

Seventeen

"JUST HOW SICK is Kara?" Eric practically accosted Vince in the locker room. "She seemed fine over the holiday, but when I went to see her at the hospital last night, she was getting tests and I couldn't go in. The nurse told me she was really sick again. What's going on?"

"It's another infection." Vince tossed his books into his locker and stripped off his jacket. "Have you talked to your sister?"

"I haven't seen her. She left for work early."

"Kara told me you spent Friday with her." Vince's statement sounded matter-of-fact, but Eric sensed resentment.

"We just hung around. Christy worked all holiday. I wanted Kara to have a good time."

"She's not some charity case. You aren't responsible for her good times."

"Hey, back off," Eric warned.

For a moment, he and Vince glared at each other. "Sorry, man. I was out of line," Vince said. "She's important to me, and right now, I'm worried about her. It's hard when you really care about someone."

Eric sighed, regretting his show of temper. He knew the way Vince cared about Kara, and knowing she'd been with Eric had to have been hard on him. He told himself he should never have gotten involved with Kara or Vince. He should have simply ignored them and stuck with his usual good-time crowd. Yet, he hadn't, and deep down, he knew there was no going back. What was worse, he didn't want to go back. Kara mattered to him. "Come on," he said to Vince. "Let's do some bench presses. I'll spot you."

Vince gave Eric a sad, imploring look. "I want her to have a good time, too. I don't want her to keep going through the ringer this way."

"Between us, we can give her a good time. Lighten up. She'll be out of there before long. She's licked it before, and she'll do it again." Yet, even as he spoke, Eric saw doubt in Vince's eyes. And fear.

Kara felt frightened. It was getting harder and harder to breathe, no matter what the doctors did. Her heart was racing, and although the cardiologist examined her and ordered medication, he didn't have any medical wonders to stop the downward turn her condition was taking. She felt lethargic, groggy, despite being on oxygen almost all the time. Dr. McGee took her into surgery and inserted a catheter in her arm for hyperalimentation—a procedure to get nourishment into her starving body more efficiently. The hospital routine around her faded in and out, and the only way she measured time was by the rattling of the food trays three times a day, the faces of the nurses as they changed shifts, and her parents' visits.

This time, Kara insisted on having visitors. She wanted to see her friends for as long as she could. She wanted to be surrounded with healthy people. Christy popped in every chance she got. As Kara worstened, her mother spent most nights in the room with her. She told Kara she'd taken a short leave of absence from her job. "You shouldn't have," Kara insisted.

Her mother's expression was obstinate. "I'd much rather be here with you. Honestly, Kara, this nine-to-five workday is totally overrated!"

"*I'm* more exciting than a high-powered position in an international ad agency?"

"No doubt about it." Her mother touched her cheek gently.

Kara smiled wryly. "That's hard to believe, but I'm glad you're here with me, Mom." Kara looked at her mother, at the worried set of her mouth, the tiny lines around her eyes. Kara just knew time was running out. She thought about the One Last Wish letter she'd received.

The letter was at home, tucked safely away in her dresser drawer. She'd read it so many times, she'd memorized it. "The miracle is not in the receiving, but in the giving and in friendships that reach beyond death."

Kara smiled to herself. She finally had the solution of what to do with the money. The answer was so simple. Kara took hold of her mother's hand. "Come closer, Mom." She patted the edge of her bed. "Sit down. There's something I need to tell you—and something I want you to do."

Vince came every day after school, sat by her bed and read to her, passages from the Bible, poetry, magazine articles, novels. If he came to an especially sexy passage, he'd stop and joke, "Now, turn your thumb down if you think your modesty can't take this."

She'd smile and hoarsely whisper, "In your dreams." Who could have a shred of modesty left after being poked and probed and examined by every person who passed through her room wearing a white lab coat?

When Eric visited, he appeared ill at ease, so Kara made an extra effort to be cheerful. Nothing she did recaptured the magic they'd shared during the Thanksgiving holiday. She longed to have him look at her the way he had that night when he'd held her and kissed her.

She understood his ambivalent reactions.

"Civilians"—people who'd never been unhealthy—were put off by her world. Hospitals weren't places for people who didn't *have* to be there. "It's nice to have you come and see me," she told him. "You've been wonderful to me."

"Maybe I'll bring my English teacher by, and you can give me a testimonial."

She attempted a laugh, but the effort hurt. "It'll cost you. I don't just toss out testimonials for nothing, you know."

He leaned over her bed and looked her full in the face. "So, what will it cost me?"

She felt the familiar sensations go through her that only he could elicit. "I'll have to think about it."

He stared at her, the look of mischievousness giving way to one of tenderness and sadness. She felt uncomfortable. She didn't want him looking at her that way. Not with pity. She broke his gaze by glancing away. "I guess I should let you get some rest," he said.

No, her mind cried. *I don't want to rest. I want you.* But she told him, "Of course. I am a little tired." She watched him start for the door. "Will you come back?" she asked, suddenly anxious about seeing him again.

"Of course," he said, giving her a puzzled look. "Why wouldn't I?"

"No reason," she said, believing there was every reason for him to stay away. He left and Kara felt an urge to cry.

* * *

"Santa's elves have come bearing gifts," Vince declared when he and Eric arrived the next day wearing Santa hats and carrying boxes and paper bags.

"What's going on?" Kara asked. She was sitting upright. Now, she slept with the head of the bed permanently elevated and her head and shoulders propped with pillows in an effort to make breathing easier.

Eric opened one especially long box and began taking out parts of an artificial tree. "Vince said you had to have one of these fake ones in your room." She nodded. A natural tree might make her wheeze.

It took them almost an hour to set up the tree, as they argued and kidded one another over the directions.

"What do you think of these?" Eric asked, dangling a long string of twinkle lights. "I've got them in all colors and in white. Which ones do you want?"

"All of them," she said. "A tree can't have enough lights." Elyse showed up with a bag of silver and gold tinsel, popcorn and cranberry chains, and hundreds of small, red decorative bows. "Are you in on this, too?" Kara asked, smiling.

"You didn't think I was going to let these two comedians handle this by themselves?" She held up the popcorn chain. "And do you have any idea how long I worked on this thing? This is an act of love, girl. I have bloody fingertips from my sewing needle to prove it."

Kara watched them work, loving them and wishing she could be helping. There had been times that she'd been in the hospital when she had been able to get up and around, but not this time. She was confined to her bed, attached to a flexible oxygen tube.

"Do you like these doodads?" Eric asked, holding up a garish display of glass ornaments.

"They're perfect."

He turned to Vince. "See. I told you she'd like them." He turned back to Kara. "He said all my taste was in my mouth."

Vince shook his head. "No—I said *if* you had taste, it would be in your mouth."

By the time the trio finished, lights twinkled, tinsel glittered, and the whole room looked like Christmas. "Wait a minute," Vince said, stepping forward with another bag and handing it to Kara. "This is for the top."

Carefully Kara opened the sack and extracted a breathtakingly lovely angel. Her face was fine hand-painted porcelain, her hair a swirl of golden curls, and her gown a cloud of white satin. "My guardian angel," Kara whispered.

Everyone watched while Vince perched the ornament atop the tree and stepped back. "Put this on the tree, too," Kara said, handing Eric the red satin pillow he had won for her at the arcade. "On the branch right below her."

He did and stepped aside. "You did great

work," Kara told them, wiping away a mist that had crept into her eyes. "Just wonderful."

"It looks okay," Eric mumbled.

Kara glanced from one to the other. "You're the best friends a person could ever have."

Elyse hugged Kara. Vince stooped and kissed her tenderly. Eric did the same, but more quickly, as if the public show of affection embarrassed him. "Merry Christmas."

Kara's eyelids were growing heavy, and a listlessness had stolen over her like a thief. "Until tomorrow," she told them, wishing she weren't so tired. Once they left, in spite of feeling tired, she couldn't sleep. She gazed lovingly at the tree. Its beauty caused a lump to lodge in her throat. She fixed her gaze on the angel and whispered, "Watch over us all, Guardian Angel."

Eighteen

ERIC HEARD THE persistent ringing of the phone. His bedroom was pitch-black, and the digits from the clock radio on his dresser glowed three A.M. He buried his face in his pillow and groaned. Finally, he heard the ringing stop and the muffled, sleepy voice of his sister. As he snuggled contentedly under his covers and sleep began to steal over him, his tranquillity was disrupted. Christy flipped on the overhead light and shook his shoulder.

"Eric! It's Kara! I'm going to the hospital. Do you want to come with me?"

Instantly, he was awake. "What about her?"

"We're losing her." Christy's voice shook. "She's bleeding severely from her lungs, and her heartbeat's erratic." Eric stared, unable to comprehend the message. *Losing her?* "I don't understand—"

Christy sat on his bed and took his hand, as one might a small child's. "I asked Kara's parents to call me if Kara took a downward turn. We're all so close . . ." Tears filled Christy's eyes, and it took her a moment to regain her composure. "Kara's lungs are too weak to keep working, and now with her heart failing, there's nothing they can do . . ."

"She's worse? But I was just with her when we decorated a Christmas tree for her room. She seemed fine."

"Eric, each day brings complications. Medically, there's just so much that can be done."

"But all those doctors—"

"They're not miracle workers. She's just too sick this time."

"She pulled out before. She will again," he insisted stubbornly, and jerked away. Eric refused to accept what she was saying.

"I'm worried about Vince, too," Christy added.

"Is Vince sick?" Eric had seen him at school that day, and he'd looked fine. Had the phone call divulged more than bad news about Kara's condition?

"He's not sick, but if something happens to Kara, he could be."

"What do you mean?"

Christy sighed. "When one of the community with a mutual illness dies, the others in the circle—especially those closest to the victim—get sicker. They give up hope. Sometimes, we lose more than one within months of each other."

Eric recoiled in horror. "But Kara won't die. She can't. This is some false alarm."

"Are you coming?" Christy gazed down at him, an urgency in her voice.

"I'll follow in my car."

"Be careful," Christy said. "There's ice on the roads."

Once she was gone, Eric got out of bed and moved around his room feeling empty and confused. He kept telling himself that there was some mistake. By the time he drove to the hospital, he'd convinced himself that Kara's crisis was a stupid error. But when he stepped off the elevator, a sickening sensation settled in the pit of his stomach.

Kara's parents were huddled together outside the door of her room. Christy stood with them, and to one side, Vince stood against the wall. Eric came up on them slowly, hearing snatches of conversation about the prognosis, as they waited for doctors who were at Kara's bedside.

Eric approached a haggard-looking Vince. "I came as soon as I could." Eric felt a need to explain himself. "What's going on?"

Slowly Vince raised his head and focused his red-rimmed eyes. "Kara's dying."

The directness of Vince's words fell on Eric like blows. He backed off. "How can you know that for sure?"

"I know."

"But I just saw her. She seemed kind of groggy, but she was talking to me."

"She was groggy because carbon dioxide's been building up in her blood. Her lungs are so shot, they can't make use of the oxygen she's breathing. Kara's suffocating to death."

Eric shuddered and felt sick to his stomach. Christy approached them and quietly said, "I've asked Kara's parents if you two can go in and see her when the doctors leave. They agreed it would be all right."

Eric felt hot and cold all over. He wasn't sure he could face seeing her in this condition. The moment the team of doctors emerged from Kara's room, Vince pushed away from the wall and headed through the doorway. Torn between staying and going, Eric looked away. Christy patted his shoulder. "Go on."

Almost against his will, Eric stepped inside. Kara was connected to machines and looked so frail. Her pulse fluttered visibly in her throat, making him think of a captive sparrow. He edged closer.

Vince was bending over her, pressing her slender hand to his lips. Her nails and lips were bluish, starved for oxygen. Eric saw that her eyes were open. Her gaze rested tenderly on Vince's face. She was unable to speak. Her gaze drifted to Eric, and she held his eyes with hers. Her face held no fear. With her gaze, she seemed to tell him, "I love you, Eric."

The unspoken words sent shivers down Eric's

spine, and his knees went weak. He felt woozy, and numbness snaked through him. For a moment, he thought he might black out. Eric stepped backward, toward the door. At the doorway, he turned and ran, brushing past his startled sister and Kara's parents.

"Eric! Wait!" he heard Christy call.

He continued down the hall, past the elevator, to the stairwell. He hit the door with a bang and half ran, half stumbled down the stairs, past landing after landing until he emerged, breathless, in the lobby. People stared as he darted past them and out into the icy cold night.

Kara felt herself drifting in and out of wakefulness. She knew Vince was holding her hand. Eric had been there, but he was gone. Handsome, strong Eric. She loved him so. Her parents stood alongside her bed and took her other hand. She felt light and airy, as if she could float right off the bed. Their hands seemed to be holding her down, anchoring her to earth.

She wanted to speak to all of them, but she couldn't. She wished they could read her mind. She would have told them, "I'm all right. Let me go." She wished for peace—for them, and for herself. She knew how lucky she was to have such wonderful people in her life. Even her mysterious friend, the benefactor who had allowed her the joy of giving back what others had given to her.

On the other side of her room, the lights on her Christmas tree glittered, piercing the darkened gloom with shimmering color. The delicate treetop angel ornament appeared to be standing on the red heart-shaped pillow, and seemed to be beckoning to her. Kara watched the angel and felt peace settle over her spirit.

Nineteen

ERIC REFUSED TO attend Kara's funeral. "How can you expect me to stand by and watch them put Kara into a dark hole?" he asked his grieving sister. "Funerals are barbaric."

Christy begged him to go. "Listen, you're wrong. Funerals give a person a sense of closure. They're a way to say good-bye one last time, a way for all of us who loved her to be together and remember her."

Remember her! Eric knew that if he lived to be a hundred, he would never forget Kara Fischer. But he couldn't stand around a cemetery and cry like a baby, either. "I won't go," Eric insisted. "I don't care if you think it's wrong. I have my own memories, and I don't want to share them."

Christy left directions to the cemetery, anyway.

"In case you change your mind," she said. "It's okay if you arrive a little late." She tried to hug her brother, but he turned away.

"I'm not going," he insisted stubbornly.

Christy went alone. Eric sat alone in the apartment feeling cold and empty. He refused to let his tears flow. He told himself he was too old to cry. Girls cried. Babies cried. He wasn't going to feel better no matter what he did.

Two days before Christmas, Christy put up a tree. "Decorating one tree this year was enough for me," he said, remembering the time he, Vince, and Elyse had set up the one in Kara's room. "I just don't feel like helping you, Christy."

"I don't feel much like it, either, but I know Kara would have wanted us to go on with the holidays. What a lousy time of year to have to bury someone you love. I feel so sorry for her parents. She was everything to them."

Eric struggled to blot out the memory of their grief-stricken faces in the hospital. Suddenly, he felt as if the walls were closing in on him. "I'm going for a drive," he said.

Christy paused from draping silver icicles on the tree. "Be careful."

"Don't keep saying that," he snapped. "I'm not a kid. What do you think I'm going to do? Explode?"

"I know that keeping your feelings bottled up inside isn't good."

"Get off my case." Eric felt angry. He knew he shouldn't be yelling at Christy, but he couldn't stop himself. "I can handle it. Life goes on, remember?"

Eric slammed out of the house, got in his car, and drove. The December day was cold and gray. Eric shivered and turned on his car's heater, then remembered it had stopped working. "Piece of junk," he snarled, and smacked the dashboard with his fist. After New Year's, he promised himself, he'd dump the car and look for another, more reliable one.

He drove past the mall where he and Vince had taken Kara the day she'd been given a pass from the hospital. He'd give anything to see her again. The desire to see her overwhelmed him. It made no sense. She was dead and buried. Gone forever.

Eric wasn't sure how he ended up at the cemetery where Kara was buried, but he did. He slowly got out of his car, zipped up his sheepskin jacket, and walked through the open iron gate. Visitors ambled along footpaths, looking at headstones and grave markers and laying flowers. He had no idea where to go to look for her. He had no flowers to leave. Nothing to give.

At the entrance was a gatehouse where an attendant was stationed to give directions to visitors. Eric's lips felt stiff as he gave the man Kara's name. He found the grave easily—the ground looked fresh and unsettled. Her marker held her name and the dates of her life span, along with the words: "And God will wipe away every tear."

Sadness swept through Eric, and he fought for composure. He sat on the cold ground, wrapped his arms around his pulled-up knees. He was startled by a voice that said, "I was wondering if you'd ever show up."

Eric turned, and faced Vince, then went back to staring at Kara's grave. "What are you doing here?" he asked, wishing he could be alone, embarrassed because he'd been discovered.

Vince crouched down. "I can't stay away," he confessed. "I come every day."

Eric stared up at the sky. Gray clouds scudded westward. They looked heavy with snow. "I miss her," he said.

"Me, too."

Eric thought Vince looked pale and exhausted. He looked too thin. "You okay?"

Vince shook his head. "I want to be with her."

"That's not such a good idea."

"How would you know?" Vince's gaze was challenging. "You didn't love her the way I did."

Eric clenched his jaw. "I loved her, all right."

"Just not enough to come to her funeral."

Eric balled his fist in the grass. "Listen. I couldn't have handled it. I cared too much about her. I would have never made it through."

"You still don't get it, do you, man?"

Surprised by Vince's tone, Eric cocked his head and looked directly at him. "What do you mean?"

"It wasn't about *you*, Eric. It was about Kara. It was about caring for her enough to show up and reach out to everybody else. Stop thinking about yourself, for once. Stop thinking about how much *you* hurt, and start thinking about how much *we* hurt."

Stunned, Eric gaped at Vince and saw raw grief on his face. A lump clogged Eric's throat. Was that what he'd done by not attending Kara's funeral? Had he been thinking only of himself and his pain. He knew Christy wept, but if he came into a room when she was crying, he would leave. Could his sister have needed him?

Eric heard Vince take deep breaths as he fought for control. "Kara loved you, Eric," Vince whispered miserably. "More than she loved me."

"Not more. Just differently." Eric wasn't sure how he knew that, but he was certain it was true.

"I used to think about marrying her," Vince admitted. "Making a home, a future, and all that stuff. Stupid, huh? Neither one of us with the life span of a gnat, but old Vince imagined we should take the plunge."

Eric recalled the night he'd held Kara in his arms in front of the fireplace. The emotions he'd felt for her coursed through him anew, making him ache. "She would have made a good wife."

Vince eyed him with a sharp, stabbing look. "You never—you know—never did anything with her, did you?"

"No." Eric looked away. He didn't add that he had wanted to. Not making love to her the night they'd been alone together by the firelight had been one of the hardest things he'd ever done. He plucked blades of brown grass. "If you had married her, would your kids have had CF?"

"Kids would have been impossible." Vince's voice had fallen to a whisper, and his face looked stricken. "Don't you know? Guys with CF are sterile. We can't ever have kids. CF girls can have babies, but not us guys."

The information all but knocked the wind out of Eric. Wasn't there anything this disease left untouched? Vince turned his head and let go a deep, hacking cough. "You probably shouldn't be sitting out here in the cold," Eric said.

"What's it matter to you?"

"It matters, Vince."

Together, they stared in silence at the ground. A cold wind rose up and swirled through the rows of headstones. Large, fat, wet flakes of snow began to hit the ground. "My mother used to tell me that whenever it rained, angels were crying," Vince said. He held out his hand and caught a puddle of wet snowflakes in his palm. They melted instantly and ran off his hand into the ground. "If that's true, they have a lot to cry about. I'll bet we'll have a long, hard winter."

Eric rose stiffly to his feet, reached down, and urged Vince up. Together, they walked toward their cars, without speaking.

It was almost dark when Eric returned to Christy's. The lights were twinkling on the tree, and the house smelled of cinnamon and warm apple cider. She practically jumped off the sofa when he came through the door. "You're home," she said, relief evident in her voice.

Eric nodded. The warmth of the room engulfed him. She'd obviously been crying, but she hastily wiped her cheeks and came toward him. "Would you like some hot cider?"

He could tell she was forcing herself to act cheerful for his sake. Her effort touched him, and for a moment, he didn't know what to do. "I stopped by the cemetery," he said. His voice sounded thick to his own ears. "Vince was there. He's in bad shape."

"And you?"

For a moment, he couldn't speak. Tears jammed behind his eyes. He tried to turn away, but Christy caught his arm and forced him to stand still. He struggled in vain against the dam of emotions, feeling naked and vulnerable in front of her. His shoulders hunched and began to heave as powerful sobs tore out of him from down deep inside.

She caught him in her arms and held him, and together they wept. Eric felt no shame.

Twenty

Eric parked in front of Kara's house and slowly got out of his car. He was surprised to see Vince's car and his sister's parked in the driveway. He thought Christy was at work. There was another car parked behind Christy's, but he didn't recognize it.

The weak rays of the January sun caught on the windows of the cars and made him blink. On Monday, second term would start at school. Christmas break had lasted too long—and had been too lonely. Eric was looking forward to returning to classes.

He rang the bell, and Kara's mother opened the front door. She wore a red sweater, and her blond hair was held back by a large black bow. She looked like a slightly older version of Kara, which momentarily caught Eric off guard. "I'm glad you came," she said, giving him a warm smile. He followed her inside.

"You said you had something to tell me," he said, then felt foolish for explaining what she already knew. She led him into the family room. There he saw Christy, Vince, and Elyse sitting on the sofa. Kara's father sat in a chair, and another chair was next to it.

"Sit down," Mrs. Fischer pointed to a spot on the couch. "You know everyone."

Eric nodded greetings, caught Christy's eye, but she only offered a baffled shrug of her shoulders. Eric realized that he wasn't the only one who didn't know what was going on.

Kara's mother passed around a plate of cookies and some soft drinks. Eric took both, not because he was hungry, but because he wanted to keep his hands busy.

Kara's mother sat beside her husband and picked up a folder from the table. "You're here because we all cared for Kara. Ted and I appreciate how much you have done for our daughter."

Eric couldn't imagine why they'd all been summoned. He shot Vince a sidelong glance, but Vince continued to stare straight ahead, ignoring him.

"We asked you here because it's what Kara asked us to do before she died," Kara's father continued.

"Our daughter loved all of you very much," Mrs. Fischer stated. "I didn't realize how much every one of you was a part of her life until her final week in the hospital."

Eric shifted uncomfortably, not wanting to be reminded of that time.

"It was Kara's last wish to do something for each of you. Kara was special. We all knew that, and someone else did, too. This person has left Kara a great deal of money." She glanced at her husband. "We've decided to keep the origins confidential, but it came from a person none of us has ever met. Knowing that someone—a caring, kind stranger—recognized Kara's uniqueness is a blessing to her father and me. All of us in this room know it, but to have a stranger recognize it . . ." Mrs. Fischer's voice caught, and Eric saw her eyes fill with tears.

He controlled himself to keep from crying. Kara *had* been special; no one could ever doubt it.

Kara's mother shifted the papers in her hands and cleared her throat. "Kara wanted her father and me to disperse her gift to you—pass it along, so to speak. With my help, she wrote down what she wanted done. I want to read her words to you now."

Eric's heart thudded, and he exchanged looks with Christy. Already, his sister's eyes brimmed with tears. Kara's mother began to read.

"I'll bet you all are sitting there feeling weird and thinking this is a scene out of a bad movie."

Everyone laughed, and the sound broke the tension in the room. Kara's mother continued.

"First of all, don't be sad on my account. We all knew I was going to die. I wish I could have had more time—especially after meeting you, Eric—but I couldn't."

Eric felt his face flush hot. He refused to glance at Vince. Eric tuned in again to Mrs. Fischer's voice.

"Unfortunately, we can't ever buy more time; we have to make the best of what we have. Miss me, but don't go overboard. That means you, Vince. I know this isn't easy for you, but you can't let it get you too far down. You've been healthy now for a while. Keep it up.

"Because you all mean something special to me, I want to give something special to each of you. My parents are behind me one hundred percent, so none of you can say no. Is that clear?"

Mrs. Fischer stopped reading and looked over at them. No one had anything to say. She looked back down at the paper.

"Elyse . . . I want you to have a shopping spree—and I don't want you to set foot in one discount store, either. Go first-class. I'm serious—I want

you to buy anything you want for as long as the money holds out. Go crazy!

"I also want you to have my art supplies. I valued them most. I know you'll take good care of them for me."

Kara's father left his chair and brought over Kara's large sketch pad and a small envelope. As he handed these to Elyse he added, "I've boxed Kara's art supplies, and I'll put them in your car when you leave. There's something in this sketch pad for you and for the others, as well as a personal note to each of you."

Elyse lifted the cover of the pad. On the top page was a large drawing of a smiling Elyse. She gasped. "It's me! And it looks exactly like me." Tears glittered in her eyes. "Thank you. I'll treasure it forever."

On the next page was a drawing of Vince dressed in his Halloween costume. He, too, was smiling and looked real enough to come off the page. Elyse carefully tore it out and handed it to a somber Vince. Vince took it and held it like a priceless crystal. Kara's father also handed Vince an envelope.

Eric's mouth went dry as Elyse turned to the next page. She handed it to him, and he stared down at a mirror likeness of himself. In the drawing, Eric was grinning and leaning against the door of his car. He'd always suspected Kara knew the vulnerable part of him he tried to hide from other people. Seeing the drawing confirmed his suspicions. It was as if she'd looked inside his soul and put it on paper. Elyse tore off the page and gave it to him. He looked up as Kara's father gave him an envelope. He saw his name written in Kara's distinctive writing style and felt a knot in his throat.

From across the room, Mrs. Fischer began to read while her husband retraced his steps and sat down in his chair.

"Now, Vince, you're next. I wanted you to have something that represents your future. You of all people know futures are hard to come by. I think that you've begun a weight lifting program that is super. But I also know how easy it may be for you to get off schedule if you land back in the hospital. So, I want you to buy yourself a home gym—a really good one that you can use whenever you feel like. Who knows? Maybe you can give Arnold a run for his money someday."

Vince sat upright, his mouth agape. "I don't know what to say . . ."

Eric remembered the day they'd been at the mall and had joked so openly about their hearts' desires. Trust Kara to remember every detail.

"And to you, Eric, I think it's about time you got that car of yours fixed up. Exactly the way you want—in mint condition. You told me once it was a classic. Now you can have it looking like

one. Spend the money and do whatever it takes to make it a winner."

Eric felt his chest constrict. *Kara,* if only he could talk to her, tell her all the things he should have said while she was still alive.

"And now, last but not least, Christy."

Eric saw that his sister was crying freely now, the tears running openly down her face.

"You were the sister I never had. Like my parents, you were there for me, day and night, anytime I needed you. Not only as a therapist, but as a friend. I can't think of anyone who deserves more from life than you, or who has more to give. I know you've always wanted to be a doctor, and that you've been saving for medical school. Well, you should be a doctor. The money I'm giving you isn't enough to send you straight through medical school, but it's enough to get you started in a big way.

"Talk to Dr. McGee. He's always been a fan of yours. He'll help you, because I've asked him to. Kids with CF need people like you. Maybe one day you'll help rid the world of CF. That thought makes me so happy."

Kara's mother stopped reading and wiped her eyes on a tissue. Kara's father reached over and took her hand.

Seeing them look at one another with such complete understanding brought Eric a sharp, instant image of his own parents. He saw his father—working thirty years in a hardware store to take care of his family. He saw his mother—thirty years by his father's side.

They were good, solid, caring parents who'd cared enough about him to challenge him, and keep him out of harm's way. Suddenly, Eric missed them. He wished he could find words to comfort Kara's parents. He wished he'd attended the funeral. He saw his desire to make peace with his parents as another unexpected gift from Kara.

He turned back to Mrs. Fischer's voice as she resumed reading Kara's letter to them.

"We come into this world with nothing, and when we leave, we can't take anything with us. I guess all we can do is leave behind our memories of what we shared. Love is more than a warm, fuzzy feeling. I think it's being totally committed to something that the heart finds precious. Each one of you was precious to me. Remember, friends are friends forever. Please stay in touch with each other if you can. Never forget me."

Kara's mother lowered her head and wiped her eyes. No one spoke. No one moved. She rose and smiled, in spite of the tears. "This gathering together was Kara's final wish. We've made out checks to you, and we want you to use the money on the things she wanted you to have."

Eric stood stiffly. The others followed. He felt numb, overwhelmed. He watched Vince embrace Kara's mother, and shake Mr. Fischer's hand. He saw Christy and Kara's mother huddle in a corner talking. Then Elyse ran over and hugged Kara's father. He wished he could reach out, the way the others could, but he didn't know how to. He was afraid if he stayed much longer, he'd lose control in front of everyone. He knew they'd understand, but he didn't want to cry.

Eric went over to the Fischers and thanked them.

"Don't be a stranger," Mrs. Fischer told him. "Please come over and visit with us. Vince and Elyse have been Kara's friends forever and always stopped by. You were obviously very dear to her. Maybe we could talk, get to know you better. Please feel that we're here for you."

"I'd like that," Eric said, almost surprised that he really did want to see them again.

"I have to go back to work," Christy told him, "but I'll see you at home tonight."

Once he was outside, Eric gulped air in an attempt to regain control of his raging emotions. He carefully laid the sketch of himself across the backseat of his Chevy. At the end of the driveway, he saw Vince standing beside his car, staring up at the sky. Eric stopped, unsure of what to do. He wanted to leave, but something inside made him hesitate. "Kara was something else,